KISS ME KILL ME

When Rosalie Bennett arrived at La Colline, the once-elegant mansion of an elderly friend known as Aunt Francie, she was seeking escape from an unhappy love affair. As the old lady's secretary and companion, Rosalie would be responsible for cataloguing her priceless collection of antiques. But then a series of frightening events occurred that convinced Rosalie that someone, perhaps the man she was growing to love, was trying to kill her!

KISS ME KILL ME

Kate Cameron

ATLANTIC LARGE PRINT
Chivers Press, Bath, England.
Curley Publishing, Inc.,
South Yarmouth, Mass., USA.

Library of Congress Cataloging-in-Publication Data

Cameron, Kate.
  Kiss me kill me / Kate Cameron.
     p. cm.—(Atlantic large print)
  ISBN 0–7927–0172–0 (lg. print)
  1.Large type books. I. Title.
[PS3553.A4334K5 1990]
813'.54—dc20

                                      89–29334
                                             CIP

British Library Cataloguing in Publication Data

Cameron, Kate
  Kiss me kill me.
  I. Title
  823.914 [F]

  ISBN 0–7451–9741–8
  ISBN 0–7451–9753–1 pbk

This Large Print edition is published by Chivers Press, England, and Curley Publishing, Inc, U.S.A. 1990

Published by arrangement with Dorchester Publishing Group

U.K. Hardback ISBN 0 7451 9741 8
U.K. Softback ISBN 0 7451 9753 1
U.S.A. Softback ISBN 0 7927 0172 0

Dedicated to
Mrs. Noble C. Cox

CHAPTER ONE

My first thought when I received the letter from old Mrs. Quentin was: *How in the world did she know? How could she possibly have known that my whole world had collapsed?* Then I recalled the words of my Great-Aunt Caroline who had been Frances Quentin's girlhood friend, 'There seems to be something strange about Francie—she seems to know about things even before they happen!' And this was long before people began to talk seriously about such things as ESP or accept the fact that some people actually *do* have some sort of a sixth sense.

I read the letter again, and it must have been the fourth or fifth time that I had done so. Suddenly, in her eighty-first year, Frances Quentin had decided that she did not have much time left on this earth. Before she lost her ability to think clearly, she wanted to begin the monumental task of cataloguing her valuable possessions and dictating her memoirs.

'Caroline—God rest her soul—', she had written, 'always said she could never understand why you wanted to become a school teacher when you were a child because you were without a doubt the best typist she had ever seen when you were just a

1

sophomore in high school. And with all those awards you won in school, you could undoubtedly have become a well paid personal secretary instead of spending your days wiping the noses and buttoning the snow suits of second graders. So I am prepared to pay you twice what you are making as a second grade teacher in Berwyn to come to North Rumford and help me with this project—which I want to *under*take before senility or loss of the ability to communicate *over*takes me. I hope you haven't signed a contract to teach next semester. I need you here.'

Was it that strange sixth sense of hers? I asked myself the question as I recalled the day in December when I had sent in my resignation to the school board. My heart filled almost to bursting with love for Kurt Richards, and I had accepted his engagement ring the night before. We were to have been married on the fifteenth of January. *Were* to have been. A slow flush of anger suffused my face and neck as the nightmare of New Year's Day flashed unbidden to my mind.

December had been one exciting night after another, filled with the magic of love. There were dinners, concerts, and long, quiet evenings when we had talked and laughed, going out for pizzas and walking in the snow eating triple-deck ice cream cones. There were days we had gone in to the Loop and

2

window-shopped and talked about preferences in furniture and china and silver. Evenings we spent poring over brochures that described in colorful phrases the glorious places we could go for our honeymoon.

New Year's Eve we had danced the old year out into limbo, and I had invited him to my apartment for dinner on New Year's Day. I wanted to show Kurt what a great little cook I was, so he could see that he wouldn't have a lifetime of delicatessen foods and TV dinners to look forward to. I felt myself to be surely the luckiest woman alive, with a handsome fiance who had made a name for himself in dentistry, a tender lover, a solid, successful man who had inherited enough money to enable him to obtain his education. He was securely established in his profession, and best of all, he was a man who wanted his wife to be a homemaker who could entertain graciously, serve on charity boards, do church work, and all those things I had always longed to be able to do. Oh, how wonderfully the vista spread before me! I loved the children of my second grade flock, but the thought of the married life that lay ahead of me was such a thrill that I could hardly believe it.

After dinner, while we were having a final cup of coffee in the living room and listening to an excellent recording of Beethoven's *Fifth Piano Concerto in E Flat*, Kurt suddenly

3

reached inside the pocket of his jacket and brought out a very official looking piece of paper.

'What's that?' I asked idly, with vague thoughts of something connected with his work, or the University, or the bank of which he was a director flitting through my head.

'It's a contract,' he stated.

'A contract?'

'Yes. It's only a couple of weeks until the wedding, you know, and I thought it might be best to bring this along for your signature, so that there won't be any misunderstanding on the part of either of us.'

'Well, for heaven's sake!' I exclaimed. 'Do you want me to promise *in writing* to love, honor, and obey?'

'Not exactly,' he said in a strangely cold voice. 'You know we agreed that we did not plan to have children because of the way we both feel about the world's overpopulation. This is an official contract that spells out our decision on this matter. I can't risk any unfavorable publicity that might be the result of annulment proceedings, so I want it in writing that you, as well as I, do not intend to rear children.'

'What are you—,' I started to say, as my eyes swept over the first paragraph of the 'contract' which was filled with a lot of to wits and wherefores and hereinafters. But it seemed impossible—oh, no, inhuman! —that

4

this man whom I had loved and who had professed to love me so dearly could have even *considered* the cruel content of the second paragraph.

'In the event,' it read, 'that conception should accidentally take place, I, Rosalie Bennett, do agree to immediate abortion. Furthermore, in the event that abortion is not deemed feasible for any reason whatsoever, I agree to carry the child to term and immediately place it for adoption in a State regulated foundling home or orphanage.'

'Kurt!' I cried, unable to read further. 'You can't mean this!'

'Of course I do,' he replied in a most matter-of-fact tone as he pulled a Sight-Saver tissue from its folder and prepared to polish his glasses.

'You mean to sit there and say you would expect me to carry a child for nine months, go through labor and childbirth, and then dispose of it? As if it were a piece of unordered merchandise?'

'I see no other way to certify that we do not in any event intend to rear children,' he said, as if it were very stupid of me to even question his ideas. 'You will also find, as outlined in paragraph three, that it has been definitely stated there will be no children adopted into our home, either. In addition to my stand on overpopulation, I don't intend to have my home cluttered with children. Mine

5

or anyone else's. They are nothing but a nuisance, and destructive little beasts, as well. I want no messy babies putting damp fingerprints on my furniture. I want no truck with babysitters, or PTAs or that kind of rot, and I want nothing to interfere with your position as my wife. Certainly no sniveling youngsters clinging to your skirts!'

I could feel the tears welling up in my eyes and a big lump of dismay swelling in my throat until I could hardly speak. The absurdity of the thing, the incredibility of it all, the out and out cruelty that must have warped the mind of this man with whom I had planned to be married was almost more than I could bear. Finally the words I had to say to him tumbled out through my numb lips and I heard myself tell him, 'Kurt, I didn't plan to have children, but this is the most—b-b-blatantly heinous suggestion I have ever heard of! Tell me it's some kind of a sick joke or something! I don't believe this!'

He replaced his glasses carefully and looked at me quite seriously as he said, 'Don't be ridiculous, Rosalie. Go ahead and sign the contract and stop being so dramatic.' He might as well have said, 'Now, this isn't going to hurt one bit. Open wider, please.'

The mirrored wall at one end of my tiny apartment reflected the scene as though it were a setting from some dark drama. *It wasn't real*, I kept telling myself. But there we

6

were—Kurt with his brown hair and eyes, his finely chiseled face, and his impeccably tailored slacks and jacket, and I with my long black hair swept back from my pale face, unbelieving blue eyes misted with tears, upper lip bearing down over lower lip. It was real, all right, and I had to accept it.

I glanced down at the two carat marquise diamond that graced my finger, stripped it off and placed it on the 'contract' which lay like an obscene blight on the dark walnut of the coffee table. My astonishment had given way to disbelief, then to cold fury as I told him. 'Take your ring and your scummy paper and get out of my apartment. I don't ever want to see you again.'

He started to mutter a mild, soft-spoken protest, but my cold fury had turned into scorching, blistering rage and I yelled at him, 'I said, get your pompous ass out of that door, you monster! Get out of here, damn you to hell!'

Kurt gathered up the ring and the miserable paper, wordlessly got his coat out of the guest closet and left. I slammed the door after him.

I was positively aghast at what I had said in the heat of my anger, for it is unlike me to use such language or allow myself to give vent to rage. Yet I could not help feeling a bit proud of myself at the same time, glad that I had shown a little backbone instead of dissolving

7

into hopeless tears. But in the aftermath of fury the tears did come, and I flung myself across the bed and cried myself to sleep.

Hours later, I began to clean up the kitchen clutter and started to think about making a list of things I had to do, something that has been a lifelong habit with me. Make a list, then act. Absently I glanced toward the living room. The placement of chairs, coffee table, sofa and lamp tables seemed to suggest a pathway that led straight to the door. It occurred to me that the furniture was not arranged in its customary position, but on the other hand I was so distraught when Kurt went out the door and out of my life that I could have picked up and set down again every piece of furniture in the apartment and not been aware of it. Glad to have something else that demanded physical action, as soon as I had set the kitchen in order I rearranged the living room and then set about my list-making.

★   ★   ★

On January 2 I called the minister of the church and told him the wedding would not take place.

★   ★   ★

On January 3 I called the school board to put

8

my name on the list of available substitute teachers.

★   ★   ★

On January 4 the letter came from Frances Quentin.

On January 5 I called the school board again and told them to remove my name from the list of substitute teachers as I was going on a trip. I then called the Quentin residence and asked to. speak to Mrs. Quentin. The voice on the other end of the line told me, 'This is Miss Erikson, Mrs. Quentin's nurse. Mrs. Quentin is sleeping, and I don't think it would be wise to awaken her unless it is urgent. May I take a message, please?'

I gave her my name and told her to tell Mrs. Quentin I would be there some time on the seventh of the month.

On January 6 I packed some favorite books, records, clothing, and a few precious pieces of Victorian glass I felt I couldn't live without, and left Berwyn for North Rumford, Ohio.

North Rumford! I hadn't been there since I was fifteen, when my mother married my stepfather and we came to Berwyn to live. Memories flooded my mind—memories of my mother and my grandmother Stet, with whom we lived. I couldn't remember my father at all because he died when I was quite small. My

Great-aunt Caroline lived with us, and it was she who had taken me so many times to visit with 'Aunt Francie' Quentin in the big old house that sat high on a hillside above the river.

My mother never liked Aunt Francie. I sensed it, even when I was a child, and asked Aunt Caroline why.

'Don't be silly, child,' she always said. 'You've got an overactive imagination.'

Then one day, when she finally felt I was old enough to understand, she told me the story.

'Francie always hoped your father would marry her daughter, Dorothy. That's all there is to it, really. Your Grandmother Bennett was all for the marriage, too, and both families simply pushed too hard. Your father liked Dorothy Quentin, and she thought a great deal of him, too. But they weren't in love—never even fancied themselves to be, at any time—and they resented being pushed toward marriage just because it pleased their parents. Well, Dorothy Quentin ran away with Hobart Willard and married him, and then your dad met your mother and married her. The dislike is all on your mother's part, Rosalie. Francie doesn't dislike your mother at all. She never did. She just figured it would be very romantic for her daughter to have married the son of her girlhood friend. And you know she has always been very fond of you.'

Oh, yes, she must have been, I thought as I recalled those days so long ago when Aunt Caroline and I had dressed in our finest and taken a cab out to the huge, rambling house on the hill far above the Ohio River. The first time I saw the place I was intrigued not only with the house itself and the magnificent view, but also with its name, La Colline, which was painted in embellished script on a name plate over the white-columned porch. Mrs. Quentin, who was probably about sixty years old then but seemed to me to be older than God Himself—for I must have been around four or five years old at the time and everyone old enough to be married—at least anyone old enough to be *widowed*—seemed surely to be close to a hundred. I told her it was the first time I had ever seen a house that had a name of its own. Laughing at my childish honesty, she asked me if I knew the meaning of the name. Of course I didn't, and she told me the full name was actually 'La Colline au dessus du Fleuve' and that the French name, meaning 'the hill above the river,' had been given to the place by her husband's grandmother who had come from Baton Rouge to marry his grandfather. I was entranced, and when I parroted the words back in some sort of an approximation of her own flawless French, she folded me in her arms and said I was a delightful child. I don't

11

think I actually remember that first trip; my Aunt Caroline told me of it years later, and she recounted it so many times during my early years that before long I thought perhaps I could recall exactly what was said. But that was the first of many times Aunt Caroline and I went there for tea, and the first of many things I learned from the gracious old lady who had been presented at the Court of St. James, had studied art in Paris and voice in Milan, owned a 'cottage' in Newport, and spent the winters with French relatives in Baton Rouge.

As I covered the miles of flat farmland and passed through or bypassed the little towns along the way, I found myself returning for long stretches of time to my strange childhood. By the time I reached Indianapolis I had decided grimly that I must have been a horrid, nasty brat of a child. I was spoiled shamelessly by my Grandmother Bennett and my elderly maiden aunt, and cosseted and treated as an intellectual equal by the greatest lady of North Rumford society. It was no wonder at all that after my grandmother and my aunt both died when I was fourteen, and my mother remarried when I was fifteen and we moved away to a city where I knew not a soul, that life seemed to close in on me and I thought I would never survive!

Miles passed and thoughts from out of the past flittered through my consciousness.

Vividly I recalled the day my grandmother died. We were visiting at La Colline and suddenly Aunt Francie had told my Aunt Caroline she had this strange feeling that Maudie was not at all well. My aunt had said she was just ready to leave for home anyway, and started gathering up her purse and shawl. 'Hurry,' Aunt Francie said, 'I'll call the cab and you must walk down the driveway and meet him.' Aunt Caroline and I walked into my grandmother's bedroom just before she breathed her last.

Then I remembered how Aunt Francie had cut short her visit to Baton Rouge and come back to North Rumford just a few days before my beloved Aunt Caroline fell victim to pneumonia. And how she cried at the funeral, and hugged me tightly, saying, 'I knew it—oh, I knew it!' That I really do remember because I was fourteen then, and I distinctly recall how she looked at me and said with a sad voice, 'Child, you're going to move away, and I will miss you so.' This was several weeks before my mother had even met the man she later married.

My thoughts shifted again to the letter, and I began to have serious doubts about the wisdom of my driving on to North Rumford. Aunt Francie had said she wanted to get this job done before the time came when she couldn't do it. Did she mean that she really knew she didn't have long to live? Could it

13

possibly be that she could foresee her own end? I didn't doubt it for one moment, and it was for that reason that I wondered if I were at all wise in making this trip. I certainly didn't want to be around somebody who was going to die. No, not I! I'm no good at all around sick people—never have been—and, if anything, I do know my own limitations. It was only because of the sickening termination of my relationship with Kurt Richards, and the overpowering feeling that I wanted to get as far away from him as I possibly could, that I was able to continue toward La Colline.

It didn't occur to me that I had failed to tell a single person where I was going until I was well past Indianapolis. I had leased the apartment the previous August, before the fall semester of school had started and had paid the rent a month in advance. I must give my forwarding address to the super when I send the rent for February, I reminded myself. I owed no bills, expected no mail. I had taken care of all my business transactions in December, winding up what I expected to be the end of my career as Miss Bennett, teacher of Grade Two, in preparation for the beginning of my life as Mrs. Kurt Richards. There was no one other than the minister to tell of the cancellation of my wedding plans. We had intended to be married very quietly in the church parsonage with the minister's wife and her brother as witnesses, and there

14

were no plans for a reception or anything of that nature. Kurt's parents lived in San Francisco, and my mother and stepfather were traveling somewhere in the Southwest. We merely had planned to write and tell them the deed was done. Now I would just simply write and tell my mother I was going to spend a few weeks with Mrs. Quentin at North Rumford, and she would learn of it when they returned to their home in Joliet and picked up their mail, whenever that might be. It certainly wouldn't make any difference to my mother, I was sure, for she and I had never been at all close since Daddy John, as I was supposed to call him, came into our lives.

That brought another distasteful vision chasing through my mind: my mother, sitting at the kitchen table, drinking coffee, looking balefully at me as I stood staring out the back door. 'What's the matter with you, anyway?' she had said with a sharp edge of anger in her voice. 'You act like John has the galloping crud or something! Don't you want me to marry him? Don't you think I'm entitled to a little happiness? I'm only thirty-five years old, Rosalie, and your father has been gone for years. I didn't even date anybody as long as your Grandma Bennett was alive, for after all, it is her house we live in, and I know it would have created some sort of a scene if I had even allowed a man to call on me—but my God! I'm a young woman, and it's not right of you

15

as if the world was going to cave in just ie I'm going to marry again!'

I couldn't tell her. I couldn't force myself to tell her how that repulsive man I was supposed to call Daddy John had run his hot hands over my budding breasts while making a big show of helping me with my coat. How I had noticed him look at me and lick his lips and rub his hand surreptitiously over the front of his trousers, with my mother right there in the room, blissfully unaware of the lascivious thoughts that I could all but see coursing through his head. I had swallowed past the lump of fear and disgust that constricted my throat and told her I was just sad at the thought of leaving the home I had known all my life, but I was sure I would like Berwyn once we had made the move. And I had smiled bravely, and kept my thoughts to myself, making certain that I was never alone with that lecherous old man. I knew that as soon as I could get away from home and go to college, I would do so—and would make sure I was completely separated from both of them from that day on.

So that's the way it had worked out. I went to college the year round, so I could complete four years of work in three. I grasped at the first teaching contract that was offered, so that I could be on my own. My Grandmother Bennett had left me a little money, and my Aunt Caroline's legacy had added enough to it

16

that I could become independent—and my mother was happy, I'm sure, much happier than she would have been had I stayed with her and 'Daddy John.'

The hills of southern Indiana began to rise and fall on either side of the Interstate. The late afternoon sun flickered through patches of woodlands and sent shafts of flaming crimson bouncing off the windows of houses and barns and flashing smartly from an occasional metal roof on my left. Those long shafts of brilliance that reminded me of the way the river used to look sometimes, just before the sun dipped from sight behind the woods to the west of La Colline.

I had hoped to spend the night on the far side of Cincinnati in order to shorten the next day's journey, but I suddenly realized I was tired in body as well as in spirit and that it would be better for me to get off the highway soon and drive on up to North Rumford in the morning. I would still be able to get to La Colline before noon, and it really didn't matter to anyone, I told myself, because I had told the nurse only that I would arrive on January seventh and had not specified a time. There had been only one thought in my mind about arriving there, and that was that I did not, in any event, want to reach North Rumford at night. The road to the house on the hill was dark and narrow and winding (at least, it had been ten years ago), and all I

17

could think of was wanting to travel that road in daylight.

A familiar blue and white sign carrying the legend 'GAS—FOOD—LODGING' caught my eye and I turned into the exit lane. Once I had made the decision to stop for the night, I began to think of the creature comforts that were clamoring for attention and wonder which I wanted most ... a long, pleasant, stinging shower? A deliciously cold martini with two olives in it? A delightful dinner in a softly-lit room, with muted music and the pleasant aromas of food and drink? A comfortable bed with crisp, clean sheets and the soft warmth of blankets? Finally I decided I wanted them all—and in that order.

After I had spent at least ten minutes in the shower and rubbed my aching body all over with scented lotion, I was ready to dress and head for that martini I had promised myself. I found the cocktail bar and sat at a table next to the wall, feeling quite wicked at being in a bar without an escort, and at the same time feeling quite insecure and uncertain. I have always been a terrible introvert and had tried for years to force myself out of the shell that college training had taught me came about because of my rather unusual childhood. So I sat there trying to look as if I were accustomed to going into a cocktail bar alone every day of my life, letting my eyes flick about the room with a studied air of detachment.

The waitress, an attractive young blonde girl with a pleasant smile, brought my drink. 'Two olives!' she said with a hint of a laugh in her voice.

'Right!' I replied with an answering smile. I lifted the glass to my lips and took an appreciative sip, and almost choked with the gasp that rose to my throat.

There was a man sitting in a booth across from me. The candlelight was dim, filtering through amber-shaded hurricane lamps, and the man was bending forward, slightly away from me, lighting a cigarette. But the line of the jaw, the dark hair, the sturdy shoulder line—all these could only belong to one person, I was positive: Kurt Richards, whom I had hoped never again in this world to see! I carefully turned my face toward the wall, hoping he would not notice me. I truly did not want to even speak to him and, above all, I hoped that despicable creature would not think I had been running after him!

I paid for my drink and started for the door, moving as unobtrusively as possible as I traversed the distance between my table and the doorway. Just as I reached the door, I felt the light touch of a hand at my elbow and stood frozen in my tracks.

'Rosalie?' A deep baritone voice sounded just in back of me.

I whirled around, a hot wash of anger

19

glazing my eyes, and there he stood, towering over me. The man who had been in the booth.

But it was not Kurt Richards, at all.

The face was similar, but the expression on it was as different as daylight from darkness. There was a brief smile, then a quick apology. 'I'm sorry,' he said. 'I thought you were Rosalie Bennett. I really wasn't trying to—'

'I am Rosalie Bennett,' I replied, 'but I don't—'

'Well, gee, I'm sure glad of that. For a minute there I thought you were going to reach up and hang one on me! I'm Bryce Willard. I used to know you when you lived in North Rumford. Are you here alone? I was just going to dinner and saw you walk past and thought surely it must be you. Imagine that! How long has it been, anyway?'

In back of me I could hear a waitress murmur to the bartender some kind of banality about it being a small world, or something to that effect.

'Would you like to join me?' I asked him impulsively.

'Yes, I'm alone, and you'll not believe this ... I'm on my way to North Rumford now. I had a letter from your grandmother last week asking me to come and do some work for her ...' We walked toward the dining room together, laughing and talking.

20

My spirits soared; it was marvelous to feel like a whole person again. I had felt as though my world, which had not been of solid construction since my early childhood, had totally disintegrated, leaving me to pick up first one piece and then another, casting away each fragment as distasteful, nauseating, confusing, monstrous, morbid. And now, here was a friend from out of that happy early childhood, laughing and talking wholesomely about people and places we both had known fifteen years or more ago.

'How is your grandmother?' I was finally able to ask.

'Not well at all. She has been a diabetic for years, you know, and spends much of her time in a wheelchair. She'd never be able to take care of herself.'

'She has a nurse, I know,' I put in, 'for she answered the phone when I called to let Aunt Francie know I was coming.'

'Yes, a Miss Erikson. Came out from Cincinnati. Big, capable woman. What was it Granny wanted you to do for her?'

'Well, she mentioned in her letter something about cataloguing her antique collection and writing some memoirs. I don't know just what she has in mind.'

'What's left of her mind, you mean. I might as well warn you that Granny has changed considerably in the past ten years. Has spells of absolute clarity and

21

then—zap!—can't remember her own name. House is in bad shape—needs a lot of repair, but she won't spend a dime on it unless something actually falls down or caves in, and won't let me do anything, either. Old man Kuykendall comes in and takes care of the furnace and screens and the yard work and stuff like that, but the place is drafty and in need of paint and—' He stopped suddenly, evidently noticing that I was swallowing hard and frowning. 'Lord, Rosalie! I've made it sound pretty grim, haven't I?'

And grim was certainly the word for it, I found out the next day.

CHAPTER TWO

It was probably because I had allowed my mind to keep drifting back to the previous night that I missed the turnoff I had carefully sketched out for myself before I left the motel room. But who could have done otherwise?, I asked myself happily when I realized that I had been day-dreaming. My moss-gathering caused me to have to cope with miles of city traffic, but somehow it didn't seem to make much difference. It had been such a warm and comfortable evening. Bryce and I had dinner together, and then he suggested we drive to an inn he knew only a few minutes away from where we were staying. There was a huge fireplace at one end of the big room, there were soft lights on snowy white table linen and sparkling glassware; an atmosphere of *Gemutlicheit* that I had missed and had not even been aware of missing.

'Rosalie,' Bryce had said shortly after we had given the waitress our orders for hot buttered rum, 'you were a sweet, attractive girl when you left North Rumford, but you have grown up to be an even lovelier young woman!'

'Oh, come on now, Bryce,' I teased. 'It's the combination of the firelight and the candlelight. I'm sure I look like any average teacher of little children.' But I glowed as much from his compliments as from the firelight, and I knew it. For the first time in a long, long time I felt that I was on safe ground. There was no constraint between the two of us. We were friends, not lovers, and I have long felt that between lovers there is a certain amount of constraint. Playing at the game of love, it has always seemed to me, requires constant watch to keep from making the wrong move, saying the wrong word, and making sure that a companionable silence becomes a conductor of unspoken thoughts for just so long and no more. But, with Bryce, there was a feeling of rapport and camaraderie, and I felt so secure that I could say what I felt like saying without being careful of nuances or phraseology that could be read the wrong way. As I made this discovery, I began to realize that Kurt had been supersensitive, so quick to slip into a black mood from misinterpreting an innocent remark—this, in spite of the horrible suggestion he later made to me in his hideous 'contract'. Bryce, on the other hand was lighthearted, happy, not uptight about a thing in the world, and it seemed only natural to me to bask in the pleasant glow, reflecting it in my own behavior.

We talked of our families. During the ten years we had not seen each other, much had happened. He asked about my mother and stepfather, and I told him they had bought a house in Joliet, Illinois, two or three years ago and were now traveling somewhere around Phoenix. I wasn't sure where.

'You were never as close to your mother as you were to your Grandmother Bennett, were you?'

'No, not really,' I admitted. 'Much of the time I felt as if I really belonged to Aunt Caroline or Grandma Bennett. My mother wouldn't allow men to come and visit her at home, but she met them away from home, Bryce. I wasn't aware of this until after we left North Rumford. All I knew was that she was gone quite a bit.'

'Well, you were thrown with older people almost as much as I was,' Bryce commented.

'My mother and father separated when I was just a baby, you know, and he took off for South America. Then my mother either jumped or fell from the Carew Tower in Cincinnati. I always thought she jumped, because what in the world would she have been doing up there on the thirty-fifth floor if she hadn't intended to jump?'

I could feel my eyes widening. 'That's one of the things I was never told about, Bryce. You know how people are with children. I was just told that your mother had died when you were little and that your father was away on business. And I never questioned it.'

Bryce sat back in his chair stiffly, a rigid expression of mock severity on his face. 'Scandal,' he intoned, 'must never sully the fair name of Quentin.' Then he broke out into a crooked grin. 'I wonder if Granny Quentin knows why my cousin Charlie never comes around North Rumford. She'd probably join the rest of my ancestors who had died of heart attacks if she knew.'

'Why, what do you mean?'

'About Charlie? Well, Charlie Quentin is gay. And about the heart attacks—you know Uncle Edward, my mother's brother, died of a heart attack, just like our Grandpa Morefield did. That was Granny's father. Seems to run in the family. Thank God I don't appear to have inherited the weakness.'

'Evidently your grandmother doesn't have

25

it, either,' I said. 'After all, she's over eighty years old. What happened to your Aunt Kathleen? Is she still living?'

'No, she passed away four years ago. Cancer.'

'I didn't know,' I told him. 'I've heard from your grandmother occasionally during the past ten years, but it has mostly been birthday cards and Christmas cards and that sort of thing, so I've really lost touch. That leaves only you and Charlie and your grandmother out of the whole family, then.'

'Well, there's my father, possibly. He hasn't bothered to write or anything for over twenty years.'

'Where does Charlie live?' I asked.

'Somewhere on the West Coast,' Bryce replied. 'San Diego, I believe. He called me at my apartment in Dayton once last year and said he was on his way to New York and would stop in and see me. I said "Come ahead, I've an extra bed," but he didn't show. Maybe he was worried about my reaction to his sex life.'

'What *is* your reaction, Bryce?' I asked him.

'Lord, I don't care.' He grinned. 'If that's the way he wants to swing, that's *his* business. Each to his own. Now me, I like girls. They're soft and cuddly and have pretty hands.' He picked up mine and stroked my fingers. A pleasant thrill shot through me.

26

Oh, it was so luxurious to bathe in the warmth of a pleasant relationship again.

I knew that if I were going to rise and shine early in the morning and drive up the river to North Rumford, I had best get to sleep before long and, much as I hated to, told Bryce I thought I should get back to the motel. He wryly admitted that he had to get an early start in the morning, too, as he had to be in Indianapolis before ten o'clock.

Driving back to Maple Grove Inn, we talked of the project Aunt Francie had in mind of cataloguing the antiques and possibly writing a history of the Quentin-Morefield families. Again Bryce mentioned that if she appeared to be a little strange, I shouldn't worry about it, for her senility was of the type that afflicts many octogenarians. It was the type that brings occasional pronounced lapses of memory and lack of control, but in between these episodes she was as alert as ever. Bryce said he made a point of going to North Rumford as often as he could get away from the demands of his business. He had invested in a Dayton manufacturing concern and was doing quite well with it. Laughingly, he admitted that his cousin Charlie called him a stuffy, stupid square, among other epithets not quite so delicate, because he was working when he didn't have to.

'But I can't be like Charlie, no way. Charlie lives off the inheritance that came to him

27

from his parents, and one of these days it'll be gone. I came into a nice comfortable trust fund when I turned twenty-one, but I couldn't see loafing my life away so I put the money to use and myself to work. The Puritan Ethic, I guess.'

'Have you—you haven't said anything about a wife, Bryce.' I felt I had to ask it. I don't know what psychologists say about it, but I feel pretty sure that even in the most innocent of conversations or relationships between men and women, the woman always wants to know the lay of the land maritally.

'I was just going to ask you the same thing, Rosalie. I've not found anyone yet that I feel like spending the rest of my life with. How about you? I don't see evidence of any wedding ring.' He was holding my left hand as he helped me from his car.

'No, Bryce, I wore an engagement ring for awhile, but decided it was a mistake.'

'Then,' he said as I reached for the door key and handed it to him, 'there isn't a reason in the world why I couldn't—,' and suddenly his arms were around me and he was kissing me tenderly. Right there in the hall. With people passing by! 'I'll be up to see you, soon.'

So I drove along, and every once in a while I had to reprove myself sharply. *Don't go reading something into a goodnight kiss that wasn't there, you darn fool! It was pleasant, it*

28

was fun, but it's not at all significant, so quit breathing so heavily and thinking about how it might feel to be romantically involved with him!

But the thoughts kept intruding, and it was not until I had to hit the brake so hard that it killed the motor when the car ahead of me slowed for an intersection that I realized such moss-gathering must stop. Cincinnati traffic was no place for being lost in romantic speculation, I told myself. Especially since the snow, which had been threatening for a couple of hours, had started to fall.

I was amazed at the changes that had taken place in the city and in the suburbs during the past ten years. Villages that I recalled as not much more than wide places in the road now stretched from shopping centers on the west to shopping centers on the east, with bedroom communities marching up and down the hills on either side of the road. Ranches and split levels hugged the new streets that swirled around through what used to be fields of corn and pasture for farm animals. Suddenly I felt depressed. What I saw was not what I wanted to see. In the back of my mind I had been looking forward to the rolling hills as they sloped down to the willows that guarded the ice bordered brooks. To an occasional glimpse of a flashing stream as it tumbled through a rocky bed toward the wide river below. To bare black trees reaching bony fingers toward the sky heavy

29

with scudding snowclouds. To cows with winter-wooly coats, to waddling families of pigs and to patches of ground sown in winter wheat. The hills were covered with raw new houses, all cut from the same two or three basic patterns, the little streams were choked with debris, and the farm land and the animals and the trees were all gone. Died in childbirth flashed through my mind. Died, giving birth to interchanges and shopping plazas.

Again I spoke sharply to my inner self: Dammit, Rosalie, you're entirely too young to resist progress! Come off it, now!

Fortunately, my sense of humor was able to lift me out of the depression that theatened to engulf me, and before long, I could look with some insight into the cause of my dismay. There's only one thing wrong with you, I said to myself, and you might as well acknowledge it. You had a traumatic experience with Kurt. The invitation from Aunt Francie came as a lifeline tossed to you in your sea of despair. You have a happy encounter with an old friend and lapped it up like a cat at the cream pitcher. Then you had yourself convinced that a return to the scene of your early childhood, a happy time in life, would be all it would take to make you a whole person again. Now you are hit right in the puss with the unavoidable truth: it is not going to be like it was then. Things have changed. Do

30

what you said you would do, get your head on straight, then light out for someplace or other and get back to teaching.

My college psychology and reproving self-analysis were to no avail. Time after time I caught myself drifting back toward childhood. The memories were too sharply etched on my mind, especially the memory of the imposing grace and elegance of La Colline.

High on the hill it sat, serenely overlooking the village nestled between the river bank and the rising highlands. The house itself had been built of sturdy Holland brick, said to have been the best available at that time. In later years the brick had been painted white, and the ornamental iron work changed from white to black. I had seen paintings of the earlier red brick with its white trim, and always thought the white painted brick much more stately. There were four large, white columns in front, reaching from the slate porch floor to the sky blue ceiling two stories above. A small balcony led from the master bedroom on the second floor, and this balcony was enclosed in curved and curlicued black wrought iron. Lacy. Lovely. Patterned after the iron work of New Orleans where the great lady visited in the winters with her relatives from Baton Rouge. There was a porte-cochere at the west side of the house, the left side as one approached it. Guests

31

drove up the private driveway from the north end of town, through an avenue of interlacing maples, then around the eastern slope of the hillside and on up to the house. The hillside itself was carefully trimmed and planted with decorative shrubs and neat beds of flowers. From Main Street far below, La Colline looked like an exotic jeweled brooch set in an expanse of emerald velvet. There was a fulltime gardener, and during the summer months the gardener's son did nothing but keep the lawn mowed and watered.

There were always flowers from the ample plantings or from the greenhouse. I could never remember a time when there were no fresh flowers in great, tall vases, their fragrance mingling with odors of furniture polish, silver polish, floor wax, and the Yardley's Lavender that Aunt Francie always wore. What was it, now, that Bryce had said about the lawn? Oh, yes. That 'old man Kuykendall' took care of it—occasionally. If it was old Sam Kuykendall that I remembered from my childhood, there would surely be little care taken, I imagined. Old Sam was a tobacco-chewing jake-legged old man who did odd jobs...

'What does jake-leg mean, Aunt Caroline?'
'Lord Sakes, child, where did you hear that word?'
'That's what Serafina Perrone said old Sam

Kuykendall had.'
'Serafina is a smart-mouth brat.'
'Yes, I know. But what does it mean?'
'It's a ... kind of disease that ... uh ... causes a sort of paralysis.'
'Does it hurt him?'
'I don't think so. Not any more.'

Suddenly I was at the west end of North Rumford. The snowflakes were swirling thicker, faster. I began to have tremulous thoughts about the condition of Quentin Road. There was sodden, gray, half frozen slush piled along the curbs, filthy left-overs from the previous snow. A door opened from a shop on my right, and steam billowed out in a misty puff. It was a concrete block, ungainly box of a building that had been painted a ghastly green, and all the windows were awash with condensation. I saw the sign, tilted at a drunken angle: LAUNDROMAT. A dreary row of small warrens housing BILLIARDS—BAR & GRILL—CARL'S CHILI—LIVE BAIT huddled together on my left, hunkered against the hillside as though bracing themselves to push back the chill that rose from the river. I swallowed hard and looked up the hill, almost afraid to raise my eyes.

'My God!' The words were torn from my lips as I caught first sight of the house from the road. La Colline, which I remembered as

33

gleamingly beautiful, a jewel crowning the top of an immaculate lawn, was a dismal, down-at-the-heel, neglected monstrosity cowering among what was left of its once magnificent trees.

Tears threatened as I looked toward the neglected grounds, the dreary house, the tangle of untrimmed trees and bushes. Even from the distance of a quarter of a mile below, I could see the sagging steps, the crumbling concrete of the porte-cochere. It seemed to me that I simply could not bear this final blow. I realized that Bryce had tried to prepare me for it, but it was just too much to accept. Through blurred eyes I tried to find the entrance to the private road, wondering all the while if my little car would be able to climb the hill. I have always felt silly driving a large car because I am so small, but right then I wished I were behind the wheel of a Mack truck.

I drove to the east edge of town and still hadn't found the entrance to Quentin Road, so I turned into a service station and inquired.

'Quentin Road, you say?' the young man in the heavy mackinaw repeated. 'You mean the road that goes up the hill to that old pile of brick up there?'

'Y-yes,' I stuttered, feeling sure the boy must believe me to be some kind of idiot. 'I used to live here in North Rumford, and I thought the driveway was ... I'm on my way to see Mrs. Quentin ... there have been so many changes ... I'm sure I must have missed it somehow...'

'Well, yeah,' the boy said as he bit at a greasy finger nail. 'That road used to run off of Main Street here between Eleventh and Twelfth, but they blocked it off when they put the new shopping center in—that's about five hundred feet on east, y'know, on accounta the traffic flow. Whatch'll have to do is go back to Tenth and take a right, go up the hill a couple of blocks, then you can pick up Quentin Road thataway. It's liable to be pretty slick up there, it's a private road, y'know, and the city don't salt and cinder it, and there's some ice left from the last snow. And it sure looks like we're in for anothern'n!'

'Yes. Well, thank you,' I managed to murmur. 'I'll try to make it.'

★　　　★　　　★

I found the road, and by careful maneuvering was able to keep the car out of the ditch. But the layer of untreated ice and deep chuckholes in what used to be beautifully maintained macadam were a constant threat to my already jangled nerves, and by the time I reached what was left of the decaying porte-cochere I was exhausted.

35

'Miss Bennett?' a voice called from the front balcony.

I looked up as I got out of the car and saw a tall, blonde woman. 'Yes,' I said. 'Where shall I park the car?' I noted the immaculate white uniform, white stockings and no-nonsense white shoes.

'Drive around to the back, if you will, please. I don't think those posts there at the side are any too solid. Oh, I'm Leslie Erikson. I'll be right down.'

I parked the car on the graveled apron in the back and brought my bags around to the front. Nurse Erikson said, 'Come in. We were afraid the storm might hold you up.'

'It hasn't been too bad until just the past few miles. Is Mrs. Quentin sleeping?'

'No, she has been down for her nap, but will be here in a few moments. Let me have one of those bags and we'll—'

She cut off in midsentence, as Aunt Francie was rolling down the center hall in her wheel chair. I would not have recognized her. She was so frail looking, I didn't see how she could even manipulate the large wheels of the chair. Her eyes, which I remembered as being amber colored, her most outstanding feature with the exception of the pile of silver hair, looked almost totally blank.

'Do come in,' she said. 'I'm so glad you could come, Alice. And so glad you could get here a little early, so we can chat a while

36

before the musicale. Miss Erikson, will you be so kind as to get Cora in from the kitchen? The other guests will be arriving and I want to see Victor, to make sure he knows where to place the carriages.'

I caught the amazed and somewhat exasperated look the big blonde nurse cast toward her patient. Mrs. Quentin had taken my hand and held it while she turned her vacant eyes toward me and the corners of her fragile lips curved into a caricature of a smile. 'This is Miss Erikson, my nurse, Alice. And Miss Erikson, this is Alice Roosevelt Longworth! Such a pleasure, my dear!'

CHAPTER THREE

For a moment I stood there, frozen, unable to think of what I could possibly say. My thoughts traveled briefly back to Northwestern University, Psychology 304, *Psychological Problems and the Geriatric Process*, and I couldn't recall a single paragraph that had been written regarding what one does when a senile person mistakes one for Alice Roosevelt Longworth.

To me, it seemed like minutes had passed before I was able to open my mouth, but I suppose it was only a couple of seconds. I have never liked to make split-second decisions—my Libra personality, I'm told—but I forced myself to say the only thing that my shattered sensibility could come up with. I smiled warmly, squeezed her hand, and said, 'Aunt Francie! It's so good to see you!'

Apparently, that was what Psych 304 should have included somewhere in Chapter 24. Her eyes seemed to undergo a color change, and the warmth crept back into them. I could easily see that her mental processes were working again, as she said, 'Oh, Rosalie! It's been so many, many years!'

'Do you know what amber is, child?'

'No, Aunt Francie. The beads are pretty, though.

Aren't they made of glass?'

'No, dear. Amber is a substance obtained from the hardened remains of what was once pine tree resin. You know what that is, don't you?'

'I think so. Isn't it that sticky stuff that sort of drips down the branches sometimes?'

'That's right. True amber is very valuable. And I'll tell you a story about it. Amber must be worn before it can be beautiful. If it just lies in a jewel box, it loses its lustre and even changes color.'

'Your eyes are like amber, Aunt Francie. I wish mine were, instead of just plain old blue.'

'But your eyes are beautiful, child. Blue

eyes with sooty black lashes and black hair, just like your daddy. He was a handsome man. You'll be a lovely young woman.'

Her amber eyes were warm and aware and shining as she told me how glad she was that I had come. 'Oh, I have so much I want to get on paper, I can't wait to get started!'

Nurse Erikson had returned with young Cora Geddie, the girl who lived down on Tenth Street and came in every day to do the bedrooms and other cleaning as well as help the cook, who had said to tell me she had put on a pot of coffee and would prepare some lunch for me, if I had not eaten. Cora was a round faced girl with round eyes to match, not unattractive, but not a raving beauty, by any means. She looked friendly however, and I was happy to see anyone with a friendly face. I told the girl that I had eaten along the way, but I would love a cup of coffee, and I'd come into the kitchen as soon as I got my things put away.

'Cora,' Aunt Francie said, 'will you help Miss Bennett with her bags? Or maybe I'd better get Sam to come over, they're probably too heavy for you girls.'

'Oh, no,' I objected. 'I didn't bring a lot of things with me and if Cora can help me for a minute we can get them upstairs without a bit of trouble. What room am I going to be in?'

'The Garland room, dear. I'll go in to the

39

kitchen and sit with you while you have a cup of coffee.'

'Fine,' I said, and followed Cora Geddie up the curving staircase. I tried to ignore the worn carpeting that traversed the stairway, the threadbare velvet that covered the banquette below the windows on the landing. The door was open into the Garland room at the far end of the upstairs hall, so called because of the wallpaper that had been hanging there since 1910. The paper itself had once been blue with a tiny white stripe. The garlands decorated the border, which was at least eighteen inches deep. The wallpaper had faded until it was more gray than blue, and the embossed roses, carnations, delphinium and daisies that had hung in deep swags from the pristine white ceiling had faded too, reminding me of pale lips and cheeks and eyes of aged women. The room was clean, the bed freshly made and smelling faintly of lavender, the crisscrossed curtains bearing evidence of very recent laundering. The dresser and bed were ornately carved walnut which had been polished to a fare-thee-well, and I couldn't understand why I felt so deeply depressed. Everything was clean and neat and in order. Yet I had an undeniable feeling of disquietude that I simply could not shake.

I glanced in the mirror as I laid my handbag on the polished dresser and caught sight of my own pale face. 'Cora,' I said to the girl, who appeared to be somewhere around twenty years old, 'I look a fright. I really do need that cup of coffee!'

'It'll probably be ready by now. Mrs. Ellett doesn't usually make coffee for lunch, you know. Mrs. Quentin is only allowed a small amount of coffee, so there's usually a big pot made at breakfast time and I always have some when I come in at eight, but she thought you'd like some after driving through that snow and sleet. And sort of unusual of her, too, I might say—though I oughtn't. Mrs. Ellett doesn't usually put herself out for anybody unless'n she's directly told to. But then again, I reckon maybe she thought with the bad weather and all...'

'Well, whatever,' I said. 'I'll just hang up my coat and be right down.'

I glanced out the window, which overlooked what had once been the formal garden at the southeast end of the back lawn. The porte-cochere took up the western end, along with the driveway which led back to the apron fronting the carriage house. There had once been a formal garden, designed in the manner of an English knot-garden with rows of annuals trimmed into an intricate pattern, and the entire area was enclosed with a boxwood hedge that had to be kept sheltered from excessive heat in the summer. The gardener had always set up portable lath

41

screens when the sun rose bright and scorching on July and August mornings. The garden, of course, had disappeared. Snow had tenderly spread a blanket over the neglected grounds, but I could see that below the snow there were no flower beds. One lonely patch of dead, brown flower heads bent toward the east proclaimed that a bunch of hydrangeas had stirred in the summer breeze, but the straggly remains had not even been trimmed before the cold winds blew down from the northwest.

Quickly I turned from the window and found a hanger for my coat, leaving everything else until later, and dashed down the stairs toward the kitchen. The view from the back window had left me as deeply depressed as all the rest of the house had. Everywhere I looked I found more and more reminders of magnificence of the past that had faded and decayed.

I used the little stairway at the east side of the house rather than the wide, Brussels carpeted stairs that rose from the entrance hall at the west side. The kitchen was directly below my bedroom, so I saw no reason for using the grand staircase. I shuddered as I ran down the wooden stairs which were covered with ugly, utilitarian rubber treads, remembering that even the back stairs had been carpeted in the old days.

I must get over this, I told myself. If I'm

going to stay here for a few weeks, as I said I would, I'm just going to have to realize that the old place has gone to pot and accept things the way they are! Cut out this silly feeling of dismay for what is gone, beyond recall!

But a tiny little voice intruded into my thoughts and said, 'It isn't really dismay, you know. It's apprehension.'

A shudder began in back of my knees and rose up along my spine and the hairs on the back of my arms responded by standing straight out. I was afraid of something. I admitted it. Some indefinable condition permeated the place so intensely that I could almost smell it. Taste it. Touch it.

Violently I shook my head in an effort to convince myself that my imagination was running wild.

'I don't want to go to church today, Mother.'

'Pity sakes, Rosalie! Of course we're going to church. Get your pink dress and let me tie the sash in the back.'

'I don't like the pink dress. It's a baby dress and it's too short.'

'Quit fooling around now and get ready. You know I hate to walk in late.'

'Can't I wear the flowered one? It wouldn't look so bad with the blood on it.'

'WHAT blood, for heaven's sake?'

'I—I don't know. Maybe I'll cut myself or

43

something.'

'You get that pink dress on and come on now, this instant. Do you hear me?'

Children, I have read since that dreadful day, often have a greater amount of insight or extra sensory perception, call it what you will, than many adults. I remembered clearly as I went down the back stairs of La Colline how it had been that day when I was thirteen. Something told me that I would come home from church with blood on my pink dress and I would be miserable. But I couldn't see that the elderly lady who sat on my right would slump forward in a stroke just as I handed her the silver tray of little glass communion cups, causing about half of them to spill their contents of grape juice all down the right side of the pink dress. Apparently I could see what was going to happen to me, but my premonition didn't include the poor old lady. She was carried out of the church and rushed to the hospital in Maysville, where she recovered completely except for an inability to use her left arm and hand. I walked home from church in misery because of the horrid purple stain that I was sure everybody in North Rumford could see. Worst of all, my mother insisted that I had dropped the communion service myself when poor old Mrs. Foxworthy fell forward, and I should have had the presence of mind enough to

44

have avoided the disaster. I wanted to remind her that I didn't want to go to church in the first place, let alone wear the stupid pink dress, but I didn't.

Coming down the back stairway I heard the creak of the wheels of Aunt Francie's chair and the unmistakable tread of the nurse coming toward the kitchen. I also heard a snatch of conversation, apparently coming from Mrs. Ellett, cut off in midair as she, too, must have heard the squeak of the wheels.

'. . . got another thought comin' 'cause I'm not a-gonna—'

I reached the back entrance into the kitchen before Aunt Francie and Miss Erikson did. Whatever Mrs. Ellett was complaining about, I decided, was not really my business and I would ignore it. I tapped at the doorway and walked on in, with a smile on my face and a hastily assumed attitude of pleasant goodwill.

'Hello,' I said. 'I'm Rosalie Bennett, and I'm sure you must be Mrs. Ellett.'

'Yes, ma'am,' she said succinctly. 'There's coffee in the pot. Cream in the refrigerator if you take it, and sugar there on the table. Just help yourself. I've got my hands in bread dough, as you can see.'

'Thank you,' I said warmly, ignoring her waspish words. 'I'm so glad you put coffee on. It was a little rough driving the last fifty miles or so. Oh, here comes Aunt Francie. I

45

thought I heard her coming. And ... isn't Cora here in the kitchen? I was sure I heard voices as I came down the back stairs.'

'Probably me a-talkin' to myself,' Mrs. Ellett acknowledged. 'Leastways, I'm accused of it all the time.'

Well, now, I said to myself, that is NOT a friendly face. Mrs. Ellett clamped her lips together and applied herself to the job at hand, ignoring me altogether. The face was lined and weathered, the lips thin, the eyes a faded blue. Her hair was an equally faded brown, pulled up into a skimpy knot on the top of her head.

I was contemplating the cook's angular frame, wondering about the advisability of trying to converse with her, when Nurse Erikson walked in behind Aunt Francie's wheel chair, a reproving look on her face. 'Now remember, Mrs. Quentin, no coffee.'

Aunt Francie sighed, her face reflecting her resignation. 'I know.' She wheeled her chair up to the breakfast nook and slid out of it and onto the red leather covered seat.

'You aren't totally confined to the chair, then,' I said, glad to see that she was not altogether incapacitated.

'Oh, dear no,' she replied. 'I just use it to keep from wasting my strength by walking. I can walk, but it tires me greatly. Now Miss Erikson,' she said as she turned toward the blonde girl who stood beside the wheel chair, 'you won't need to stay with me. When Rosalie has finished her coffee we'll go into the sun parlor, and you can bring my four o'clock medication in there. Until then, if you have anything you want to do, errands to run or anything of the sort, why go right ahead.'

'Very well, Mrs. Quentin,' the nurse said and turned to go. 'Just be sure you don't overdo. And you must rest for an hour before dinner.'

I heard the steady tread of the nurse's oxfords as she went up the carpeted staircase toward her own room. A door opened and closed in the upstairs hall, and I asked Aunt Francie if Miss Erikson had the room next to the master bedroom. She sighed.

'Yes, the one at the top of the stairs as you go up. The price one has to pay for growing old, it often seems to me, is having to practically give up one's privacy. Edith's room is on the other side of me. I have never disturbed the suite of rooms at the far end of the house where Edward had his study and the library. Now you are in the Garland room, next to the library, and the library is open, dear. The study is the only room that's closed. There are three other guest rooms at the back of the house, you may remember, but we don't have many guests any more, so they are rarely used.'

'But you used to have a lot of company, Aunt Francie. When I was just a little girl I

47

remember seeing the house ablaze with lights up here. There were musicales and charity teas—and I believe the drawing room was used for piano recitals, wasn't it?'

'Oh, my goodness yes. The Chamber Music Society met here for years, and the Longfellow Club, too.'

'Aunt Caroline told me that many years ago there were balls held here that were really fabulous! The Spring Cotillion, the Masquerades—oh, that must have been a very romantic time!'

'Yes, and Caroline was such a beauty. She could have married royalty. Did you know that?'

'No!'

'Oh, yes, she could. There was an Austrian Count who came to the Christmas Ball one year ... he was absolutely smitten with Caroline but she would never consider marrying him. He was a handsome fellow, too. I can remember as if it were yesterday, his polished manners, his elegant coach with its coat of arms encrusted with jewels. How beautiful Caroline looked dancing with him...'

'Why wouldn't she think of marrying him, Aunt Francie?'

'Oh, she said that with the exception of loving to waltz, she had nothing in common with him. Such a pity.'

Aunt Francie's mind seemed to travel

distant roadways into the past and I was afraid if I didn't say something quickly and get her to think of the here and now, she'd look at me again and not know who I was.

'Uh ... is anyone living in the carriage house?' I asked.

'Hmmmm? ...' With a wistful smile she returned from that far place where her mind had roamed. 'Oh. No, no one, now. Victor passed away several years ago, poor man, and I just decided it wasn't worth while to maintain a car and a chauffeur on the place for the few times when I feel like going out. Miss Erikson has her own car, it's the red one that's parked down on the apron, I imagine you noticed it as you came in. She goes in and out quite a bit, and doesn't bother to put it in the carriage house. Edith—Mrs. Ellett—doesn't drive; whenever she needs to go anywhere she takes a cab. And Cora rides with the Webster boy who works in Maysville. He drops her off in the morning, that is, and she walks down the hill at night. It isn't really far to where she lives, if you cut through the property down where the plum thicket used to be.'

'Used to be? No plum thicket any more?'

'No, not any more. Got to be too much trouble. People don't want to go to the work of making plum butter when they can buy it in the store.'

'Yes, I suppose so,' I said. I finished my

49

coffee and again told Mrs. Ellett how much I appreciated it. Then I poured another cup for myself and took it into the sun room. We talked of many things, and time passed quickly. It was four o'clock before either of us could have believed it, and Miss Erikson came in with the medicine and a carafe of water.

'You must rest before dinner, now, Mrs. Quentin.'

'Yes, I'll go up immediately.'

It hurt me to see this once strong figure of a gracious lady placed in total submission to the orders of a nurse. At the same time, another thought struck me. 'How do you get up the stairs in your chair?' I asked.

'Bryce insisted that I let him put an elevator in for me, Rosalie. It's been put in here where the large coatroom used to be, off the drawing room. There was plenty of space, and since we don't have the crowds of people here that we used to, nobody misses the coatroom at all. The elevator takes me right into my bedroom, you see, since it's directly above the drawing room.'

'Fantastic,' I commented, thinking how considerate of Bryce it had been, and when Miss Erikson returned to the sun room, I mentioned it to her.

I was surprised at her caustic reaction.

'He's just after the old lady's money, Miss Bennett. Does everything he possibly can to ingratiate himself with her. Comes popping in every few days, usually with some silly gift like a bunch of daisies or a book of cartoons. Lord! I can see right through him.'

'Oh, really?' I said, and I could feel my eyebrows arching all the way up to my hairline. 'I would imagine Aunt Francie would get a lot of pleasure out of little things like that. Most of her friends have all passed away, and it's sure to be lonely for her.'

She snorted. 'Well, that's true, of course, but what he ought to do is make some repairs on this dreadful house. You look out the windows at the stair landing and you can see what a bad shape that porte-cochere is in. Why, you saw it yourself when you came in. Those stone blocks look as if they could fall down any minute. And that disreputable old man that comes in to check on the furnace and shovel the snow—why, he doesn't earn half of what she pays him—whatever it is!'

While Nurse Erikson was berating old Sam Kuykendall I began to notice a strange quality to her voice. A hint of an accent? And if so, what is it? Rather British—but yet not exactly. I tried to identify it, and finally gave up and came right out and asked her. 'Where are you from, Miss Erikson? Somehow I have a feeling that you aren't an Ohio Valley native.'

'From Canada,' she replied. 'Took my nurse's training at the University of Toronto.

Came to Cincinnati to visit a friend, and decided I'd register for private duty. I rather like it here, really.'

'Have you been here with Mrs. Quentin very long?' I asked.

'About eight months, more or less.' She rose from the couch where she had been sitting, straightened out the pillow and abruptly said she would see me at dinner. 'Did anyone think to tell you that we dine at seven? Mrs. Quentin likes to be in bed for the night around nine.'

'No, she didn't tell me. I guess it slipped her mind. I think I'll go up, too,' I said. 'I'd like to take a good, hot shower and get into something decent.' I thought about the empty coffee cup and decided I'd better take it to the kitchen. Mrs. Ellett hadn't appeared overly friendly and I was sure she would not take kindly to cups or glasses being left here and there about the house.

I watched the trim figure of the nurse as she swept up the staircase and wondered what it was about her that I disliked. Yes, I admitted to myself, I do dislike her! I tried to convince myself that it was just her disparaging remarks about Bryce; or maybe it seemed to me that she looked at Aunt Francie with a loosely veiled threat in her eyes; or maybe she was just a bossy female, accustomed to giving orders and brooking no nonsense from anybody. And bossy females have never been among my favorite people. Then I considered how sad it had made me feel to realize Aunt Francie was unable to make decisions for herself, and rationalized that my dislike of Miss Erikson was because of her aura of authority while Aunt Francie was placed in a submissive position. Defense of the underdog came to mind.

Well, no, I reproved myself. Underdog was not the right term. And while I was trying to straighten out my thinking, the horrible day the police closed in on poor old Ferdie Gilroy came to mind.

When I was nine years old and in the fourth grade at North Rumford Elementary School, I was walking home from school one afternoon when I happened to see Ferdie Gilroy shambling down the street toward me. Ferdie Gilroy was a victim of elephantiasis. People said it was remarkable that Ferdie had lived beyond childhood with his hugely distended fingers and toes that protruded from pudgy hands and bulbous feet. His lower arms and lower legs were equally hideous, swollen so badly they were mottled and the skin had a shiny, bruised look to it. Ferdie was somewhere in his early teens; no one seemed to know, for Ferdie's mother kept completely to herself, living on the pension she received as a widow of a railroad man, and caring for Ferdie who everyone said was mentally defective.

My Aunt Caroline once told me she didn't think there was a thing wrong with Ferdie except that getting to and from school was such a problem that somebody along the line decided he was uneducable. Besides, nobody expected him to live so they figured there was really no use in spending money to teach Ferdie anything. Looking back, I could see that Ferdie was quite retarded socially, but in all probability if he had been born twenty years later and lived in a place where special education classes were available, he might have had a chance.

At any rate, Ferdie Gilroy was used by many ignorant mothers as a threat to keep recalcitrant children in line. 'Ferdie Gilroy'll get you if you don't behave!' 'No, you can't go outside to play—it'll soon be dark and old Ferdie Gilroy might be around.'

Ferdie usually stayed in his own yard; probably he feared the taunts and namecalling of loutish children who had never been taught by their parents that such behavior is brutal and disgusting. Once in a while he would slip away from his mother's watchful eye and wander down the street. Ferdie never wandered far: the mere act of putting one foot in front of another was a painful accomplishment, and his physical impairment kept him close to home as well as his fear and distrust of society. But on this particular day he had managed to traverse the two blocks between his mother's house and Tenth Street, where I saw him shuffling along.

Suddenly I heard the sound of pounding feet on the sidewalk in back of me and stepped aside to let whoever was in such a hurry run on past me. The scurrying feet belonged to two burly policemen who were heading toward poor Ferdie Gilroy with revolvers in their hands! As I stood there in Mrs. Martin's driveway, open-mouthed, a patrol car bore down toward the frightened boy. I didn't know whether I wanted to scream, or cry, or run into the street and be sick. Ferdie Gilroy wouldn't hurt a soul, I knew! And there were all those policemen converging on him.

Before any violence or rough handling could have taken place, young Mary Belle Farnsworth came out of the butcher shop at Tenth and Main and calmly told the policemen she would see that Ferdie got home all right.

That, I had to acknowledge, was what it was about Miss Erikson that I didn't like. Authority using the implements of authority or the commands of authority when it really wasn't necessary. It appeared to me that Miss Erikson could have spoken to Aunt Francie with a little more kindness, a little more consideration.

My inclination toward self analysis then led me to wonder if perhaps I had transferred my feelings of anger from Kurt Richards to Leslie Erikson. Not that there was any similarity between the two: Kurt dark, handsome, virile; Miss Erikson blonde, efficient and female. Kurt had represented professional authority and I had never thought of questioning any of his decisions until the debacle of New Year's Day. Perhaps there was enough of a carryover of the appearance of professionalism, I conceded, that could cause me to resent what I felt was the nurse's high-handed treatment of my old friend.

When I walked into the kitchen, Mrs. Ellett jumped, dropped the spoon she had held in her hand, and looked up from the pan she had been stirring. 'Didn't hear you comin',' she said accusingly as she retrieved the spoon from the floor. 'Don't like to have people sneak up on me like that.'

'I'm sorry,' I said. 'I certainly didn't intend to sneak, Mrs. Ellett. These shoes that I wear to drive in have rubber soles, and they don't make much noise. Really, I didn't mean to startle you. The h-house is awfully quiet, isn't it?' I stammered, wondering if I was expected to ask permission to enter the kitchen. She grunted a monosyllabic reply, and I continued, 'I thought I had better return this cup before I go upstairs. I've got to take a shower and get some of the dirt of the road off my body.'

I scooted up the back steps, hoping the sour old woman wouldn't throw the cup at me, and headed for the bathroom. Unpacking could wait, I figured.

I did take time to get out a robe and some clean underthings, but that was all. I found towels and a fresh bar of soap, pinned up my hair and started the water for a luxurious shower. Nothing is more relaxing to me than being able to rub soap all over my body and then let the sharp, stinging spray rinse it off.

Standing in the shower, I tried to sort out the things that had been disturbing me. There was poor old Aunt Francie, alert one minute and off the next. There was Edith Ellett who seemed to be mad at the world, or was she angry because of an additional person to cook for? There was Nurse Leslie Erikson, whom I did not like and couldn't quite decide why. There was La Colline, a splendid mansion that had turned into a shabby shambles. The thought of the decaying old house was enough to break my heart, but I knew I would simply have to accept it.

Suddenly a scream was torn from my throat as the warm, relaxing shower turned into a scalding inferno of steam. My arms, shoulders, breasts, stomach and thighs were painfully burned before I could turn off the hot water tap. As I reached, I realized that there was not so much as a trickle coming from the cold water faucet.

I could no more keep from wailing in anguish than I could have deliberately stopped breathing. I got out of the tub, patted myself gingerly with the towel, and looked in the medicine chest for some kind of ointment. As I was searching for Solarcaine, Dermassage or something of that nature, I heard Miss Erikson come running down the hall. 'What's happened, Miss Bennett?' She was calling. 'Are you all right?'

Finally I got a towel around me and opened the bathroom door. 'Somebody tried to scald me to death,' I said, sobbing in pain.

'Oh, dear,' she said. 'Let's get some cold towels on you. Now you just climb into bed and I'll wring some towels out of cold water and that'll be the best thing for the burn.' I was in such abject misery that I didn't demur at all. I didn't even resent her take charge attitude. I simply got in bed and let her minister to me. She took some plastic bags from garments that were hanging in the clothes closet and placed them over the cold towels she had carefully positioned over my scalded skin, then drew the covers up over me. The terrifying thought raced through my mind: She knew I was going to take a shower. Did she somehow turn off the cold water and try to scald me, then have a change of heart and decide to try to make me as comfortable as possible? Or was it Edith Ellett, who had given me that fisheyed look and accused me

58

of sneaking into her kitchen? I had mentioned to her that I was going to take a shower. Or was it merely the plumbing in the old house that desperately needed overhauling?

My mind seemed to be roiling and churning, trying to come up with some kind of answer. Dimly, I heard Leslie Erikson ask me if I had any tranquilizers.

'Blue plastic bag on dresser,' I mumbled.

She found the bag, located the little vial of green and black capsules and brought me one along with a glass of water and an aspirin.

'Here, now;' she said, as a mother would speak to a small child. 'You take these and drop off for a while. I'll hang up your dresses and things for you. If you want to rearrange them later, why, do so. At least they'll get the wrinkles out.'

Through my half-closed eyes I could see it was actually my own medication and an aspirin I held in my hand, not some poison calculated to bring me to a quick death, and within a few minutes I could feel the pain diminish and my shrieking nerves relax. In a hazy world of half sleep I heard Miss Erikson removing dresses, skirts and blouses from my large bag and hanging them in the closet. Then she leaned over the bed and said softly, 'I've plugged in your electric clock that was in the bag with your dresses. The alarm is set for 6:30. That'll give you enough time to get ready for dinner. Now you sleep for a while.

I'll close your door.'

I turned the worrisome thing around in my mind for a while, examining each facet. *Was it an accident, or was it intentional? And if it was intentional, who did it . . . and why?*

But the feeling of tranquility was beginning to smooth out the jagged edges of worry, and shortly I began to think, Oh, the hell with it! and slept.

CHAPTER FOUR

When my hazy mind was finally able to grasp the fact that my alarm clock was trying to tell me something, I reached out an arm in automatic response and for a brief moment had that 'Where am I and what am I doing here' feeling. Then it all flashed back, and I found myself returning to the incident of the shower and Miss Erikson's competent treatment which brought almost instant relief from the pain. In spite of my instinctive dislike of the nurse, I certainly had to admit that she knew what she was doing; and for that, I was most grateful.

In the mirror I could see there was still a little redness across my upper back, but that was the only place that showed the effects of the scalding hot water. I had expected to find big puffy blisters all over my skin.

Quickly I found a bra and pantyhose, applied a minimum of makeup, slipped into a soft blue polyester frock, ran a comb through my hair and was ready. As I walked down the grand staircase, I wondered if dinner at Aunt Francie's would be like dinner had used to be, or if the Madeira linen tablecloth had given way to one made of plastic lace.

'Why is it called Madeira?'
'Because the embroidery work was done by women who live on the island of Madeira. Notice how skillfully it is done. The reverse side is almost as perfect as the outside.'
'Where is the island of Madeira?'
'After dinner, Rosalie, you may go to the upstairs library and look it up. You are nine years old; that's old enough to find something in an encyclopedia. Find out where it is, and find out what else is exported from the island.'

As I entered the dining room, I closed my eyes for a moment in silent thanks that this one room remained untouched by the ravages of time and neglect. The huge cherry dining room furniture was still there, complete with fine old linen cloth on the table, candles in silver candelabra, sterling flatware and the complete setting of Block and Fan pattern of Victorian glass. There were no fresh cut flowers to grace the table, but a pot of red geraniums had been placed on a large Block

61

and Fan plate and the bright crimson of the blossoms was reflected in each facet of the glittering goblets, sugar bowl, creamer and butter dish on the table.

'How perfectly lovely, Aunt Francie! It's just like I remembered it.'

'I knew you would not have forgotten the dining room, Rosalie. You used to say it was your most favorite room in the house.' She indicated that I was to sit at her right. Miss Erikson sat at her left, and Mrs. Ellett sat at the foot of the table.

'Well,' I said with a smile, 'why shouldn't it be? There's the same marvelous view of the river from the big window here that there is in the living room, and there's all the gorgeous glass in here!'

'Are you still as enthusiastic about the Victorian patterns as you used to be?' Mrs. Quentin laughed, and her amber eyes twinkled with golden lights.

'Yes, indeed,' I replied. 'And I was just thinking—that's another of the many things you taught me. Like how delicious a puff of salted whipped cream can be on a bowl of tomato soup. And how to arrange flowers in a vase to show each bloom to an advantage. And the Madeira linens. Do you remember when you decided I was old enough to use the library and find out about Madeira wine?'

She laughed happily, and little spots of color touched her withered cheeks. 'Oh, yes!

I believe you were somewhere around nine or ten years old, and I thought if I let you have just a taste of Madeira wine you would associate it with what you had learned about the linen and you would remember it.'

Mrs. Ellett snorted. 'You mean to tell me you let a little ten year old child have a drink of wine? I wouldn't a-done that, a-tall!'

'Well,' I said mildly, 'it was a very graphic lesson. And I'm sure it made much more of an impression on my mind than it would have if some geography teacher had stood up in front of a class and said, 'The island of Madeira is one of a group of islands under the Portuguese influence, located northwest of the coast of Africa. It is noted for its export of wines and fine embroidered linens.' Wouldn't you agree, Miss Erikson?'

'Of course,' the nurse said. Did I imagine it, or was there a look stronger than mere disagreement that flashed between the two of them? Mrs. Ellett got up from the table and went to the kitchen to replenish the gravy bowl. 'By the way, Miss Bennett,' the nurse continued, 'are you feeling all right after your ... uh ... misadventure?'

'What's that?' Mrs. Quentin inquired, her face immediately reflecting her concern.

'Oh—' I hesitated. I hadn't intended to bring up the subject at dinner, but I couldn't think of any quick way to avoid it. So I just blurted out what had been on my mind. 'I

63

was taking a shower, when suddenly the cold water was turned completely off somewhere in the house. I thought I would be boiled alive before I could get the hot water tap turned off. Miss Erikson heard me cry out. It was while you were napping before dinner, Aunt Francie. She put some cold compresses on me, which really did do the trick. I'm very grateful, Miss Erikson.'

The cook had returned to the dining room with the gravy bowl and before she set the bowl back down on the table, she looked sourly at Mrs. Quentin and said, 'The water pressure in this house is terrible. All a body has to do is run enough water to peel potatoes in and you can't even get a drink out of an upstairs tap. You ought to have Sam look at them pipes, Miz Quentin. Maybe get the Jones boys up here to work on 'em some.'

As Mrs. Ellett was speaking, a strange glaze seemed to wash over Aunt Francie's eyes, which such a short time before had been sparkling with interest and recollection of happy times in the past. Her chin sagged downward, her eyelids drooped at the outer edges, even her nose seemed to become pinched and white. Her voice, when she spoke, was like the echo of words borne on a desert wind. 'In ... the ... spring...'

A subtle change had taken place, I realized, but hoped it was only momentary and turned my attention to the delicious dinner.

64

Whatever I may have thought about the antisocial behavior of the cook, I had to admit that the dinner was excellent. A roast, succulent and well seasoned, bright orange carrots and a salad made with fresh spinach leaves, all prepared to perfection. I noted that Mrs. Quentin's plate had been prepared in the kitchen, and recognized that her food must have been weighed. I started to ask her if she still enjoyed good food as she used to, and if she were greatly restricted as to what foods were permissible, when I noticed she was looking at me as if she were not sure who I was or how I happened to be sitting at her table.

'Now let me see, dear,' she said. 'Did I meet you at the Taft Tea, or was it the Hospital Board meeting? I just can't—'

I heard Nurse Erikson murmur, 'She's confused. Just play along with it until she finds herself again.'

Oh, no! I thought. *I don't want to be here. I can't stand to watch the disintegration of a fine mind. I'll leave. I'll leave in the morning. This is no place for me.* Aloud, I managed to say that we had met many times, then turned toward the cook. 'That was a really delightful dinner, Mrs. Ellett.'

Mrs. Ellett grunted, but the monosyllable seemed to be a little more gracious than her usual response, and then she said, 'There's ice cream for dessert. We usually don't have

65

anything extra like pie or cake, because of Miz Quentin. She can have the dietetic ice cream, see, and it don't bother her none thataway.'

After dinner, I volunteered to help clear the table, but Mrs. Ellett assured me she didn't need any help, so I went into the living room with Mrs. Quentin. I had no idea how I could converse with her, for I didn't know whether her mind was in the present or back somewhere around World War I.

As I walked to the south side of the living room, which was lined with windows to present the view of the sloping hillside and the river in the distance, I decided I had better stick to something safe, like the weather. When it is clear the view is magnificent, the hillside is fringed with trees at the bottom, and the trees form a screen which conceals the sordidness of the village below. What the eye picks up is the wide sweep of the river and the lavender-to-gray shades of the Kentucky shore. I decided to make some comment about this to see if it might create a spark of interest in the mind that had apparently slipped so far away. 'It's snowing awfully hard,' I said. 'I doubt if you could see the river for the snow.'

For a moment, there wasn't a sound in the room except for the sonorous ticking of the huge grandfather clock. Finally the wispy voice broke into the silence and she said,

'Edward died ... when it snowed ... his heart, you know ... by the time the doctor could get up the hill, he was gone.' And the voice, too, was gone. It had trailed off into nothing.

I stood at the window, not knowing just what to do. Should I try to get her to remember me? Would it do any good? I settled for small talk, mentioning how much I knew she had always loved Edward, then in a lighter voice went back to the view from the windows. 'Such a gorgeous panorama spread below the house. Really, I don't know which is prettier, the summer with the river shining like a silvery-green ribbon below the village, or the winter with snow blanketing everything.'

There was no word from Aunt Francie in the wheel chair. I turned to see if she had fallen asleep, and just as I turned my head away from the window, I thought I saw the lights of a car going down through the long driveway below. Surely no one could have come up the hill, turned around and gone back down without being noticed by somebody! I must have been mistaken. It must have been a reflection from somewhere—with the snow coming down like this, things become distorted. It could be far down in the village below.

Miss Erikson came in and said it appeared that Mrs. Quentin had dropped off to sleep.

'She often does this, you know, when she loses contact with reality.'

It saddened me to see how fragile my old friend was in mind as well as body, and I told the nurse that I had thought she was quite well in the afternoon when we had talked in the sun parlor until after four o'clock.

'Yes, that's true,' she replied. 'But there's the possibility that the excitement has been a little much for her. I rather imagine I'd better get her to bed for the night. I understand you know your way around the house quite well, Miss Bennett, so feel free to read or watch television or whatever you wish. Mrs. Ellett will see that the house is locked for the night after she finishes in the kitchen, then she will no doubt go up to her room. I have some letters I must write, so after I get Mrs. Quentin to bed, I'll be in my own room. I'll see you in the morning.'

Her words carried no edge, they were not spiteful, they could not in any way be considered discourteous, but to me it appeared she had simply stated she wanted to concern herself no longer with me and was consequently removing herself from my presence. I was irritated. I was still angered and hurt by her officious behavior toward poor Aunt Francie. 'Go to bed. Take your medicine. No coffee. Don't overdo. Eat your dinner. Do as you're told.' Yet I had to admit that if it had not been for Miss Erikson's

68

speedy action, I would in all probability have suffered painful blisters from the scalding water of the shower. I vacillated between dislike of the nurse and trying to bring myself to believe that she was a capable person, merely doing the job she had been trained to do.

'Uh, wait a minute, Miss Erikson,' I said. 'When do you think it would be best for Mrs. Quentin to work on the cataloguing project she has in mind? Does she usually feel better in the morning, or in the afternoon? I think I should get some kind of a working plan set up.'

'Oh, in the afternoon, by all means, if she's able to do anything at all. She usually sleeps until eight or eight thirty, then has her breakfast and bath, and reads her mail and the morning paper. That takes up the greater part of the morning, and lunch is served at twelve thirty. Then she has a short nap, and she may feel able to dictate whatever it is she wants to work on from around two o'clock on.'

'That'll be fine,' I said. 'That'll give me mornings to get the dictation from the previous day typed. I believe I'll go back in to the dining room now and see if there have been any new pieces of glass put in the cases since I've been here.'

'D'you really go for that stuff, too?' Miss Erikson twisted her upper lip into a

69

disdainful moue. 'Mrs. Quentin thinks it's the greatest thing in the world. Me, I wouldn't have it. Wouldn't want the trouble of keeping it polished.'

'Oh, I love it just as she does!' I exclaimed. 'Each piece is like an old friend.'

'Better not let Ellett hear you say that,' the nurse said. 'She has a fit every time the bloody goblets have to be washed. Has to put a turkish towel in the bottom of the dishpan and another on the counter top, and if ever she dropped one, there'd be fair hell to pay.'

Poor Mrs. Quentin sat there in the wheel chair, mentally adrift, while the nurse pushed her toward the elevator. 'Goodnight, Cornelia,' she said as she suddenly opened her eyes and turned toward me. 'I must get a good night's sleep, because Edward and Kathleen and little Charlie will be here tomorrow. Have you met my daughter-in-law, my dear? She's a lovely girl, and little Charlie is a darling boy. But the ... the ... handle came off the ... uh ... vase ... or was it the chlmfprm ... uh ... luh ...'

I smiled and waved goodnight while I could have cried at her meaningless mumblings. Edward and Kathleen had both been dead for many years, Charlie had not been to see her for ages, and she had called me 'Cornelia.'

Poor soul, I thought, and turned again to the front window and looked out into the night. Where the large rectangle of light from

70

the living room windows was thrown against the snow-covered lawn, I could see the big, fat flakes falling, slanting toward the ground. And there was my little car out there in all that snow, I thought. Why hadn't I had the sense to put it in the carriage house? Well, because I had taken a shower and darn got myself burned alive, that's why. I decided it was useless to bother with it before I went to bed, since inches of snow had already fallen. I'd take care of it the next day.

When I returned to the dining room, it was as though I were returning to a sanctuary. There was a warmth there that did not exist anywhere else in the house, with the possible exception of the kitchen. And that, I assured myself, would have been a much warmer room if it were not for the truculent disposition of Mrs. Ellett. I laughed as I recalled the expression one of the kindergarten teachers of Clayton P. Eberhart School had used, referring to Miss Cramden, our principal: 'She looks like she must drink vinegar for breakfast instead of coffee.' But I told myself to be charitable—after all, the poor woman could have troubles of her own.

Aunt Francie's collection of Colonial and Victorian Glass and her priceless pieces of Art Glass were housed mostly in two large built in closets. They flanked the cherry buffet on the east wall of the room, and each closet, covered by two huge glass doors, was at least

71

six feet wide and reached from the floor to the ceiling. As a child, I could, and often did, spend an entire afternoon just looking at the pieces and seeing if I could remember the names of the patterns. I wondered if I still remembered them! It was the Pattern Glass that intrigued me the most, although the pieces in the Art Glass cabinet on the right were really much more beautiful. Along the shelves of the Art Glass cabinet were pieces of satin glass in pink, blue, green and yellow; one whole shelf of milk white edged with open-work, some with velvet ribbons run through the scalloped and slotted edgings; a collection of animal pieces; gorgeous Peachblow, Amberina, Aurene, cased glass of all kinds, and some Stiegel glass that was reputedly made around 1770. This was so precious that I scarcely dared look at it for fear it might break, but even so I still liked the Patternware better.

As I stood there and admired the polished pieces that reflected the light from the ornate chandelier, it occurred to me that I preferred the patternware because each one had a name. I had been entranced by names from the time I was a small child. The fact that the house itself had a name delighted me, and then when I found that each goblet on those shelves of the left-hand cabinet had a name of its own, it gave me a feeling of pure rapture. I stood there, enchanted as I had been long years ago, recalling the names of the patterns.

Ashburton—the oldest in the collection, with deep, round, connecting planes.

Bellflower—with vining, trilobate flowers traversing the verticle ribs.

Cane—that really does look like chair caning translated into glass.

Daisy and Button—familiar to more people than any other pattern, because there are so many reproductions, but this one unmistakably authentic.

Eggs in Sand—with clear oval figures lying against the sand-like stippled background.

And so on, at least one for each letter of the alphabet.

The shelf below held another alphabetically arranged set. These were the patterns that bore names of people. There was one called Bryce, which had given young Bryce Willard no pleasure at all when he was a little boy, and one called Rose in Snow which I had claimed for my own, as it was the closest to my own name. I remembered some of the other ones: Henrietta, Eva, Ruby, Anderson, Patricia. The next shelf held bowls and compotes that carried state, city, and other 'place' names. Here were Ohio, Kentucky, Indiana, Texas, Wheeling, Richmond, and many others.

Above the shelves of goblets was a shelf of spoonholders, all of different patterns. I admired the intricate design of Opaque

73

Scroll, the charming simplicity of Diamond Point, the dazzling Diamond Sunburst which flashed in red, the graceful elegance of Beaded Swirl, the ordered clarity of Nailhead. Yes, without a doubt it was like meeting a host of old friends, regardless of what Miss Erikson thought! But then I had to remind myself that I had acquired a taste for this particular type of beauty at a time when I was easily influenced. And I didn't need to be told that the few pieces of Victoriana I had acquired for my own private collection were, as much as anything else, tangible links with the part of my past that I liked to recall.

I crossed to the priceless display of Art Glass in the righthand china cabinet, and noted two pieces that I did not recall seeing there before. One was a small cutglass vase, rococo in style, cut and decorated in such a manner that I thought surely it must be the work of Christian Dorflinger. The other was similar to the pictures I had seen of Venetian glass designed by the great artist, Ballarin. My mind quickly seized on these two pieces for use as a conversational wedge to get Aunt Francie back on the path of sanity, should she wander from it again.

As I stood there, traveling back and forth in time from the pleasant past to the troubled present, a strange feeling began to possess me. A chill worked up my spine and out through my shoulders and arms. *Someone was watching me!* Quickly I ran to the window and pulled the cord to draw the heavy gold damask draperies. The cord broke in my hand!

I ran to the kitchen, thinking Edith Ellett's scowl would be preferable to unseen faces in the dark. Mrs. Ellett wasn't there.

The back door was locked and the kitchen was clean, everything had been put away, but there was no sign of the cook. I tried to convince myself she had gone up to her own room, but then I remembered that Miss Erikson had said Mrs. Ellett would be around to lock up everything for the night, and I was positive that she hadn't been through the dining room, living room or the hall. I didn't want to go upstairs, leaving the place wide open to anyone who might have an eye on the valuable paintings, the tapestries that hung in the drawing room, the silver, or, most precious of all as far as I was concerned, the antique glass collection! On the other hand, I was nothing less than panic-stricken at the idea of remaining downstairs alone.

I cowered in the hallway between kitchen and dining room, afraid to move in any direction. My hands seemed to be out of control. I found myself first pressing a hand against my lips, then cupping the fingers of one hand into the other, my arms tight against my body. *Should I scream? Oh, of course not! It's only your imagination, you stupid*

75

coward. There's no one out there in this weather!
And Mrs. Ellett is around here somewh . . .

There was a noise in the back stairway. I stood frozen against the wall of the wide hallway, wishing frantically that I could find some place to hide.

CHAPTER FIVE

With my heart thumping madly, I stood there and awaited whatever fate had in store for me. My imagination had run rampant, and I could visualize a burglar who had sneaked in while I was in the dining room, slipped up the grand staircase and methodically killed the occupants of one room after another—Miss Erikson, Aunt Francie and then Edith Ellett—and was now coming after me. I heard no shots. *He must have stabbed them all to death! Oh God! I don't want to die that way—all bloody!*

I thought of dreams I had had in the past of being faced with extreme danger and unable to move my feet and legs. That was exactly the way I felt. I couldn't so much as open my mouth to scream. It was almost as though I were suspended in time and space, too terrified to even breathe deeply, lest someone hear me.

I felt my legs turn to jelly and slid to the

floor as I saw Mrs. Ellett's unsmiling face and angular body come through the back doorway into the kitchen.

'Lordamighty, girl!' she screeched and came flying toward the hallway. I must have been bleating something about being afraid everyone in the house was murdered, in reply to which she gave me a disgusted look and said, 'Miz Quentin and the nurse are upstairs, and I had to go to the bathroom, for heaven's sake!'

Finally I was able to drag myself to my feet and stumble up the back stairway to my room. In the back of my mind had been a half-formulated idea of spending some time in the library, but I quickly decided against it. I realized I would probably be scared to death in there, too. Ashamed of myself for being so stupid, and tired from the long drive anyway, it seemed to me that the best thing I could do would be to bolt my door carefully and get in bed. Then I remembered that I still had my belongings to put away, and was actually grateful for the task that would keep me from thinking about other things. I pulled the shades and busied myself with underthings, cosmetics, books and records, and lovingly removed the bathtowels I had wrapped around my three prized pieces of glass: A Tulip pattern pomade jar, a Rose in Snow plate, and a lovely Fleur de Lis cruet. Although it was my intention to get away from La Colline as soon as possible, I have never been able to abide clutter, and after everything had been cleared away and my suitcase neatly set alongside the dresser against the wall, I knew I would feel more settled and ready for sleep. So after I had put everything in drawers and rearranged the dresses and skirts that Miss Erikson had hung in the closet for me, I set my three exquisite pieces of glass on the dresser, smiled and acknowledged them for the security blanket they represented to me, and prepared for bed.

I had expected to be unable to sleep, because of the confused thoughts that persisted in tumbling through my mind, but apparently physical and mental exhaustion were more powerful than fear and disquietude, for I fell asleep almost as soon as my head touched the pillow.

But it was not an untroubled sleep; I awakened shortly before midnight when the wind began to rise and howl through the leafless trees that surrounded the house. Intermittently I dozed, but even as I slept I was aware of the brutal wind. At one time I got out of bed and looked out the window. The fat, fluffy flakes were no longer drifting down in big puffs as they had been earlier in the evening. The snow had changed to hard little pellets that rattled like machine-gun fire against the windows from the northwest. Occasionally there was a strong gust of driving rain, or a mixture of rain and sleet. The house creaked and groaned as the cold attacked its arthritic joints, and I shivered and jumped back into bed, pulling the spread up to my chin. In a few minutes, I had to remove the spread and put it back in place at the foot of the bed, and admit to myself that I wasn't really cold, it was just the combination of the weather, the old house, and the freaky feeling that I had of somebody—or something—being out there watching. Marking time until some dreadful deed could be accomplished.

I turned over on my stomach and tried to get back to sleep, and was just drifting off toward that plateau that precedes deep sleep when I was brought to my feet by a loud, resounding crash.

Feeling that surely the house must be tumbling down all around me, I dashed out the door and ran down the hall toward Aunt Francie's room. There was no light there, and no sound coming from within. I listened at the door of Miss Erikson's room, and heard nothing there, either. Then I tiptoed back and stood for a second in front of Edith Ellett's room. There was no evidence of any light there, either, but the sound of her snoring was somewhat comforting.

By that time, I was certain I wouldn't be able to sleep any more for the rest of the night. I flicked the bedside lamp switch, and nothing happened. 'Damn!' I muttered. The power had evidently failed. I should have realized it, I thought, because this has always been a problem in the North Rumford community. Just let a storm come along, and the power goes off.

Again I went to the window that faced out over the back yard and tried to see if I could see anything besides the freezing rain. The night had that gray, opaque look that is caused by heavily white clouds. The moon was almost totally obscured by the cloud layer, but once in a while the veil was flipped away from its face and a flash of white light slanted toward the earth. In one of those rare glimpses of moonlight that illuminated the back yard, the gravel apron and the carriage house beyond, I glanced toward the rear of the house and saw a huge, hulking object where I had left my car. Don't panic, I commanded myself. It's not anything supernatural. It's probably something blown against the car. A branch of a tree, maybe.

Too terrified to go downstairs for a closer look, and unable to read because of the power failure, I slipped back into bed and pulled the covers up over my head. When I awoke the next morning, the bedside light was on in my room, and a glance at the electric clock told me it was ten after three. But I could see it was daylight outside, so I was sure the power had been off for hours. I threw on a robe and went back to the window, wondering if I could make out what it was that had blown against my car. The snow had stopped sometime during the night, and everything was beautifully covered with soft, deep drifts of white. Everything, that is, except my car. It was covered with a heavy sycamore tree that had blown over on it, and from the window I could see that a large limb had landed squarely against the hood.

'Oh, no, no!' I wailed. Realizing that I couldn't cope with Aunt Francie's failing mind, a nurse that I instinctively disliked and a cook that seemed to dislike me, I had fully intended to write a note to Bryce and mail it to his Dayton apartment, then head back for Berwyn again as soon as I could get my things together in the morning. Now those plans could not be carried out. The first thing I would have to do would be to get a wrecker up there to get the tree off the car, then I'd have to find out how extensive the damage might be to the motor, probably have to have the windshield replaced, God knew what all, and I would be forced to stay until the car could be repaired. Oh, how I regretted that quick decision to come to North Rumford where I thought I could be at peace in a world that held no threats! A world bounded by the walls of a gracious old home that held treasures from the past and excluded all that was crass, sleazy, contemptible.

81

Glancing at my watch, I noticed it was actually a quarter past eight, and felt that I had to have a cup of coffee even though it did mean putting up with the sullen face of Mrs. Ellett. This was one of those times when I truly wished I had learned to enjoy a cigarette; for if they calm people's nerves as they say they do, then I needed one. Bryce had told me he had cut down to only six cigarettes a day. He had told me I should be glad I'd never acquired the habit. Recalling his words and how pleasant the evening had been in his company was soothing in its effect and before long I was able to slip into a pair of slacks and a sweater and trip down the back stairs, listening for sounds of movement in the kitchen and sniffing the air for the hoped for smell of coffee. This time, I took great pains to make a little noise as I descended the steps, so that the dour Mrs. Ellett could not accuse me of sneaking up on her.

She was sitting at the kitchen table, coffee in hand, looking so cross I was almost afraid to speak.

I had determined to be pleasant, no matter how I felt after my wakeful night and the disastrous storm. 'Good morning, Mrs. Ellett. Did you see what happened to my car?' I said as I poured a cup of coffee for myself.

'Yes, I did. You shouldn't have left it out. I

don't know why that nurse leaves hers out all the time, either. Miz Quentin told her to run it in the carriage house, but she says she'd rather have it here where it's handy. Too dang lazy to walk an extra fifty feet or so, I reckon. Trouble with the world today. Ever'body wants to walk right out of the house and get in their car. Downtown section don't amount to a hill of beans anymore 'cause people won't walk nowhere. Got to have a shoppin' center where they can load up groceries into a cart and then drive up and load it into the car.'

'Well, time, or the lack of it, enters into it,' I said as reasonably as I could. 'Perhaps when Miss Erikson has a chance to get away for a few minutes, she wants to make every minute count. And I simply forgot about my car yesterday, after the incident with the shower. Then when I did think about it, it was quite late and had already started to snow, so I decided to let it go until this morning. Now I guess I'll have to call a garage. Oh! I certainly hope my typewriter didn't get smashed along with the hood!'

'Sam'll be up before long to shovel off the snow. He always comes in for a cup of coffee, so I'll ask him to see if he can get it out for you. Car locked?'

'Yes, I did lock it. Force of habit, you know. In the city I wouldn't have dared leave the car unlocked. I'll get my keys and leave them with you.'

She gave me a strange look, at least I thought it was strange, and said, 'You got yourself into a heap of trouble by comin' here, didn't you?'

'Well, so far things haven't quite worked out as I'd planned,' I admitted. 'It'll cost me quite a bit for body work on the car, for one thing, and—'

'No tellin' when they can get it fixed, either. Paper hasn't come this mornin'. Guess the truck can't get up the hill. I don't know whether Cora'll be able to get here or not, but that kid she rides with, he's got chains on his car so maybe she'll make it. Sam, he lives in a trailer over in back of the greenhouse. Miz Quentin felt sorry for him, livin' down there close to the river, and told him to get his trailer set up there on her property. Won't know a thing about anybody till the phone gets back in order—'

'Oh, is the phone out, too?' I wailed. 'I know the power has been off. Did the storm keep you awake?'

'Didn't hear a thing,' she said. 'Didn't even know they was a storm till I woke up. Slept right through everything, tree a-fallin' and all.'

I was amazed. How could she? I figured she was lying. She didn't like me, she wanted me out of there for some crazy reason or other. Yet I tried to convince myself she was

84

just a sourfaced old woman, not a monster plotting some murderous scheme. After battling with my sense of outrage for a second or two I blurted out part of what I had been thinking: 'I don't see how in the world you could have slept through it! I was awake half the night.'

'Well, for one thing,' she said reprovingly, 'I'm not a scaredy cat, in any way at all. I always say if they's somethin' that can be done, why, do it; but nothin' can be done about it, you just have to put up with it. Now,' she pushed her chair back and indicated she had nothing further to say to me, 'I've got to get Miz Quentin's breakfast tray ready. Miss Erikson will be comin' in to check on it, and after she takes it up to her, then I'll fix you some breakfast.'

'I can fix my own, Mrs. Ellett. All I'll want is a piece of toast.'

'You need more than a piece of toast, missy. And I'll fix it.'

Why should I let this old battle-axe intimidate me, I asked myself. I told her I was going into the living room and look at yesterday's paper, for I had not seen a newspaper or listened to a newscast the day before, having been on the road all day.

I picked up my coffee cup and went out toward the front of the house and was drawn to the wide expanse of windows overlooking the hillside and the river far down below. The sun was breaking through the clouds and illuminating each twig and weed which was enclosed in an icy sheath. The myriad flashes of light hurt my eyes, and I looked back toward the partial shadow created by the shrubbery and the Corinthian columns of the porch.

'Why are they called Corinthian columns, Aunt Francie?'

'Because they are the most ornately carved of the three types of Greek architecture. The people in the Greek city of Corinth long ago developed this heavily ornamented style. See the carved leaves at the top? The tops of the columns are called capitals, because they are the heads of the columns. "Capital" comes from the latin word "Caput" which means "head."'

'But what are the other two kinds? You said there were three.'

'Look up "capital" in the encyclopedia and come back and tell me. Then get a piece of paper and a pencil and show me what all three look like.'

The acanthus leaves had crumbled in many places, revealing a ragged appearance which I had not noticed the day before, because of the snow. And as I looked out again over the unblemished white hillside, I noticed something else close at hand I had failed to see at my first morning glance.

There were footprints out there.

My stomach curled up in a tight little knot. There actually had been somebody prowling around the night before! Somebody had been watching me while I was in the dining room!

I was torn with the desire to tell somebody, either Mrs. Ellett or Miss Erikson, that there were footprints out there, but I feared appearing brainless and stupid. Besides, I realized with a sinking heart that I didn't really trust either of them! For one stunned moment the thought struck me that maybe it was Aunt Francie who had been out there. After all, she could walk, and although she had ostensibly gone up to bed, she could easily have slipped back down the elevator which connected her room with the downstairs drawing room, quietly slipped out the door and around through the snow to observe what I was doing. Oh, that was absurd, I told myself. Aunt Francie wouldn't—no, even with her sadly twisted mind, Aunt Francie would never be capable of doing such a thing. Besides, common sense pushed such ridiculous thoughts aside and reminded me that in all probability Nurse Erikson had administered medication to assure that Aunt Francie got an untroubled night's sleep.

But the NURSE could have used that elevator and slipped around to spy on me ... I tried to shake myself out of such paranoid thoughts and decided I would simply go back to the kitchen, using the excuse of returning the cup I had taken with me, and mention to Mrs. Ellett that I had seen footprints out in front, noting the reaction my words would cause.

When I reached the kitchen, I found old Sam Kuykendall sitting at the table. I hadn't heard any sound at the back door, and while I had heard a murmur of a voice in the kitchen, I had assumed it was Mrs. Ellett talking to herself again and thought nothing of it.

Sam jumped up and shook hands with me. 'It's good to see you, little Rosie! Will you be staying long?'

'Nice to see you, too, Sam,' I replied. 'Looks like I'll have to stay longer than I had planned. Did you see what happened to my car?'

'Yep, I noticed that. Edith tells me you've got a typewriter in there you want me to get out if I can.' He sat back down and ran his gnarled hand over his balding head. A lifelong habit, I recognized, of smoothing back hair. When I was a little girl, Sam had had sandy colored hair that had a tendency to fall forward, and he rarely stood up or sat down without passing a hand over his stubborn locks. Now the hair was practically gone, and he had in many ways changed greatly from the way I remembered him, but the habit was still there. Sam's face was gaunt and crisscrossed with lines, and his shaggy eyebrows were almost white. But there was a twinkle in his brown eyes that time, pain, and loneliness had not erased.

Impulsively, I decided that old Sam Kuykendall was my best bet for someone in whom to place my trust. 'Sam,' I said, approaching the subject rather gingerly, 'there are footprints in the snow out in front of the house. Last night I had the feeling that somebody was looking in through the windows, and thought it was just my imagination. But now I see there really was someone out there!'

Before Sam had a chance to say a word, Mrs. Ellett snorted. 'Sam made them tracks hisself, child. He come around past the front and up to the back door while you were goin' from the kitchen into the livin' room with your coffee.' I looked toward her as she spoke, then back to Sam, and thought I saw a faintly curious look on his face. Had I imagined it, or was she telling him that those were his footprints? And if so, who was she covering for?

'That's right,' he quickly said. 'I thought I'd better take a look around the front to see if any damage had been done by the storm. Then I came on around to the back. Now, I'll go out and see if I can get your typewriter out of the car for you, then when the phone gets back to working again you can call the Three-Point Garage. That's your best bet. They've got a tow truck that can make it up the hill here. Some of the rest of 'em, I don't know about. Be sure to tell them there's a tree limb across the car. They'll need an extra chain and a helper to move that big limb. That's a damn shame, honey.'

'It's all I can do to keep from bawling like a baby, Sam,' I said. 'My car didn't have a scratch on it!'

'Well, it sure has now,' he commented, but there was a world of sympathy in his words. 'Looks to me like it's going to need a paint job, besides a new windshield. And they'll likely have to order the windshield from Cincinnati. North Rumford never stocks anything. Always have to order it.'

'I told her what she should of done,' Mrs. Ellett said as she turned around from the kitchen range, 'was to put the car in the carriage house.'

I bit my lip to keep from expressing my opinion of people who always have to bring up what should have been done, and turned to go back up to my room. It was in my mind that I should write a note to the supervisor of the apartment building in Berwyn to let him know my address, in case anyone should happen to inquire, and send him a check for the next month's rent. But Miss Erikson came into the kitchen with a tray just then.

'Miss Bennett,' she said, 'Mrs. Quentin would like for you to come up to her room this morning for a while. The morning paper hasn't come, and the mail delivery will probably be late, she believes, and she feels like doing some work on her cataloguing project. I'd suggest you go now, while her mind is clear. She's had her breakfast and bath and seems to be quite well.'

'Thank you,' I said. 'I'll go right up.'

Sam went out to see if he could manage to extricate my typewriter from the damaged car, and as I left the kitchen in back of the nurse, I heard Mrs. Ellett call to him just before he reached the back door. 'Wait a minute, Sam,' I heard her say very softly.

That did it! I was now positive that Edith Ellett and old Sam Kuykendall were in cahoots on something or other, Mrs. Ellett obviously wanted me off the place, and the tree limb had fallen on the car so I couldn't leave under my own power to keep from being frightened to death. Now I was sure that she and Sam were going to have to cook up something else, some other way to get rid of me.

But why? The question continued to plague me.

I walked up the staircase wondering how long Mrs. Quentin would remain lucid, and then it occurred to me that my own sanity was at stake. I wondered how long I could cope

91

with the fears that beset me, especially considering the fact that there was no place for me to go. I knew no one else in North Rumford, and there was nothing I could do but wait until I could use a telephone, get a wrecker up the hill, get a windshield replaced, and get out of the house.

Of course I could have put on my coat and walked the mile and a half down the winding road to Tenth Street, then possibly located a cab and gone to the garage, but finding a cab was an iffy sort of thing considering the weather. I had promised Aunt Francie I'd help her with the work she wanted done and I didn't want to go back on my word. If it had not been for Aunt Francie who, when she was herself, was the dearest friend I had, I would have left La Colline the day I arrived.

Besides, I told myself as I wavered between dashing out into the snow covered world, bag in hand and leaving my car, my only possession of much value, and remaining in the house with its inherent threats, if someone had been watching me—as I was sure was the case—what was to keep that person from tracking me down, lying in wait, biding his time until I made a foolish move or left myself wide open for attack?

As I knocked at the door to Aunt Francie's bedroom, another thought flashed through my mind. There was something I hadn't given the slightest consideration to before, but the fact presented itself like a sharp needle that pricked my consciousness. *How did I know Bryce wasn't involved in this mess?*

I had seen headlights below the house last night, but I had tried to convince myself the lights were farther down the hill than I figured them to be. But Bryce could have driven part way up the drive, left the car there and walked the rest of the way, gone into the basement and eavesdropped at the kitchen doorway. Perhaps he heard me say I was going to take a shower, and then cut off the cold water at the outlet pipe in the basement as soon as he heard the water running! And it could easily have been he who was outside the dining room window tramping around in the snow. I realized he had told me he had an appointment in Indianapolis, and couldn't possibly have driven from Indianapolis to North Rumford by nightfall after meeting a customer for lunch but, on the other hand, how did I know that he had actually gone to Indianapolis? He could have merely told me that, when in actuality he was intent on coming to North Rumford with the idea in mind of scaring me away from La Colline.

I gasped in dismay, with my hand ready to knock on the door, when I realized I could have been made a perfect fool of by his apparent friendship, his flattery and his warm, sweet kiss! But why would he have any

93

reason to want to get rid of me? I pondered that question for a flicker of an instant and came up with a most obvious answer: he might have thought that Aunt Francie intended to leave me some of her money. He might have believed that the reason she summoned me from Berwyn was to have me with her at the end. But then there was something else I forced myself to admit: he might have thought I had trumped up the letter from Aunt Francie and was going on my own to La Colline with the idea in mind of trying to inveigle Aunt Francie into leaving some of her fortune to me!

I swallowed hard and knocked again at the door.

'Come in, Rosalie.' The frail figure was sitting up in bed, a pink bed jacket over her shoulders. 'I don't feel quite up to going downstairs this morning, but there are a few things I want you to write down for me. Open that little desk over there and you'll find some note-paper. I want you to get a supply of paper and a pen and sit down here next to the bed.'

The little rosewood desk was just as I remembered it, on the south wall between the wide window and the French door that led out to the balcony. I located the catch that opened the desk, found the note-paper, picked up a pen from the tray, and came back to the chair which was placed close to her

94

bedside, saying, 'The snow is beautiful outside, Aunt Francie. Don't you feel like getting up long enough to look out the window?'

She raised her fragile hand and waved it carelessly to one side. 'No, dear, I've seen a lifetime of snows, and I want to get started on this work. I want to begin with the collection of Sandwich Glass, which has been designated in my will to go to the Cincinnati Art Museum. There are several things I want to make a note of. Then I want to make some notes on the Aurene, Burmese, Peachblow and the rest of that collection. This is going to a museum in Marietta. And there is much history connected with the collection of glass hats, which will go to a museum in Baltimore.' Then she said, as though she considered what was to me such a mind blowing statement did not deserve additional comment: 'It isn't necessary to categorize or catalogue the Pattern Glass, my dear, because it's all going to go to you.'

'Oh, no!' I protested. 'Aunt Francie, it's far too valuable. I'd be happy to have you put my name on one piece of it, if you'd like, but please don't think of anything more than that!'

'Hush,' she said. 'It's already in the will. Has been there for over twenty years.' From under her pillow, she drew out a key chain holding two keys. 'It takes both of these keys

95

to open the cabinet. It's a double lock mechanism. I want you to take these keys and keep them. Now, no tears, please. We won't spend any more of my valuable time discussing it, because I want to get on to the Sandwich collection. I can remember each piece as it sits on the shelves in the dining room. I don't need to even look at it to recall its history. The Sandwich shelf is engraved on my memory as indelibly as the faces of my husband and my three dead children, Charles, who only lived to be three years old had fine blond hair and big blue eyes. If he had been born now, instead of then, you know, his life could have been saved. It was a congenital heart defect, and now they're doing marvelous things to correct such problems. Edward also fell victim to a heart problem when he was only twenty-six and young Charlie was a baby. Dorothy, poor girl, was so beautiful—' She stopped abruptly and said, 'I'm wandering. Now, write this down:

'The Quentin collection of Sandwich Glass was acquired through descendants of John Kugelhoff, who was associated with the Boston & Sandwich Glass Factory during the time when Heinrich Kalb was working there. Each piece is authentic. First I will discuss the epergnes, which are placed in the back row of the top shelf of the cabinet on the right, as one faces it, or on the south end of the east wall. At the far left is an epergne which appears to be quite simple, but I want to remark on the fine craftsmanship of the piece. At the base...'

The voice was not much more than a whisper, and I had to strain to make sure that I caught each word. My own thoughts were crowding in on me. They hammered home and reinforced the fleeting warning that I had tried to give myself but had not wanted to accept, that Bryce perhaps suspected his grandmother intended to give the Pattern Glass collection to me. Although he had absolutely no interest in the glass for its own sake, it would bring a considerable amount of money if it were sold. Bryce might intend to stop at nothing to scare me away from the place. He might have in mind making sure that I sign over my interest in anything bequeathed me by Aunt Francie. By threat, or by snuffing out my life so that I wouldn't be around to inherit anything. In that way, Bryce and, of course, Charlie, wherever he was, would be sure to acquire everything that was not expressly willed to museums.

My fertile imagination went into action and I could see in my mind's eye an antique dealer's impassive face offering a flat figure for the entire contents of the Pattern Glass collection. Bryce stating in a businesslike way that the figure was much too low. The dealer increasing his bid. Finally the dealer loading the precious pieces into a station wagon while Bryce Willard and Charlie Quentin split the money.

My heart would not accept it. I could not convince myself that Bryce was in any way involved in the curious set of circumstances. The only thing was, I knew I cared more for him than I wanted to allow myself to, and I was sure there was more than the mere resumption of childhood friendship in his feelings for me.

Quickly I brushed aside tears of anger, dismay and confusion, and paid strict attention to the voice of the mistress of La Colline.

CHAPTER SIX

In a most businesslike way the thin, wispy voice continued to describe each piece of glass on the top shelf of the Sandwich and Art Glass collection cabinet. The elderly woman knew the history of each vase, candlestick and lamp as well as who made it and when. Suddenly, shortly before eleven o'clock, her eyelids drooped and she sank back against the pillows. 'I'm very tired, Rosalie, dear. Let's continue this project this afternoon after lunch. I'll rest for a while now. Oh, you'll need some place to put your typewriter, and

I'd suggest the library.'

A light tap sounded at the door, and Miss Erikson came in with a tray of medication. 'I'm afraid she's tried to do too much,' she said, and gave me a disapproving look.

I told the nurse I hoped not, and said that Mrs. Quentin had indicated she wanted to continue the work in the afternoon.

Aunt Francie opened her eyes, which she had closed when she lay back against the pillows, and smiled as she looked at me. 'No, I don't think we'll get much done this afternoon. Bryce is coming.'

Before I gave a thought to the out of order phone, I said, 'Oh, did he call?'

'No,' she said, and again waved the fragile hand nonchalantly. 'He couldn't have. The phone's out. But he's coming. I know.'

My heart began to thump uncontrollably. The part of me that wanted to accept his friendship, and possibly his love, rejoiced. I did want to see him. It had been such a happy evening I had spent with him, and I could not deny that my very body was hungry for love. Oh, Bryce, I thought, it would be so easy to love you! Then the other part of me, the sensible part that expressed disapproval of my tendencies toward romanticism, told me that I was seventeen kinds of a stupid idiot, and if Bryce did come that the best thing for me to do would be to keep out of his way. As if she had some magic power to look inside my head and read my mind, Aunt Francie again opened her eyes, smiled, and said very softly, 'Bryce is a good boy.'

I returned her smile as warmly as I could when I felt like whimpering and taking flight, said, 'Yes, Aunt Francie, I know he is.' Then I ran down to the kitchen. The typewriter was sitting on the end of the counter, and through the back window I could see Sam was still there, shoveling the snow beyond the porte-cochere. Mrs. Ellett told me Sam would carry the machine wherever I wanted him to put it. I told her I would probably be working in the upstairs library, and would appreciate it if he would take it up there for me.

'I'll call him in right now,' she said. 'I want to get the dang thing off the end of my counter.'

'Just tell him to put it on the desk up there,' I said. 'I'm going in to the dining room to check some of my notes.'

I heard her walk heavily to the back door and call, 'Sam!' as I went through the hall and into the bright dining room where the table had been laid for lunch. Figuring I would have an hour or more to review my notes, I pulled up a chair in front of the right display closet and checked the individual pieces of glass as Mrs. Quentin had described them. I could not see an inaccuracy anywhere. It was amazing to me that she had such perfect recall that she could see each piece in its place without even looking at it. Even so, common sense reminded me that she had had much of this collection for over sixty years, and it was quite reasonable that she knew each piece and its history by heart.

While I was sitting there, checking my notes against the contents of the shelves, I heard the telephone ring and Cora Geddie's young, clear voice as she answered it. That the phone had rung meant only one thing to me: that I would now be able to call the Three-Point Garage and have them come up and get my car. But I could not help hearing Cora's pleased giggle and her joyful 'Okay,' just before she hung up the phone. Boyfriend, I thought, automatically.

But in a few minutes Cora came into the dining room with a big wide smile on her face and announced that Mr. Willard was going to be there for lunch. I had not even been aware that Cora had come in until I heard her answer the phone, and asked her if she had had any trouble getting up the hill. 'A little bit,' she replied. 'I didn't get here till almost eleven. Donnie couldn't get his car started so I walked up.' She went to the china closet on the south wall that held the Limoges china and the Fostoria glass which were used for informal occasions and got out another place setting. Cora placed china, glass and silver on the table carefully and grinned as she said, 'And boy, am I glad I did get here!'

'Why? Are you fond of Mr. Willard?' I asked. 'You seem to be quite happy that he's coming for lunch.'

'Oh, yes, I sure am,' she replied. 'He's real good to old Mrs. Quentin, for one thing. And for another thing, Mrs. Ellett's in a better humor when Mr. Willard's around. I thought I saw his car go down the hill past our house last night, but I guess it wasn't him. He wasn't here late yesterday, was he?'

'No,' I replied. 'He had to see someone in Indianapolis yesterday.' But I shuddered inwardly at the thought that possibly Cora did see Bryce's car. That perhaps I really did see car lights going down Quentin Road. Then it occurred to me that if Bryce were bent on getting rid of me, he surely wouldn't do anything in front of his grandmother and the cook and the maid and the nurse! So all I had to do would be to make certain I was never alone with him. Never give him any kind of an opportunity to do away with me!

Cora was chattering away and I realized I hadn't been paying much attention to her, being so absorbed in my own desperate thoughts. '—did you know Mr. Willard when you used to live in North Rumford?'

Apparently she had asked the question before, and I hadn't heard her. I pretended to have been carefully checking my notes, making a few check marks deliberately before I answered her, then looked up and said, 'Oh, yes. I used to come to La Colline quite frequently with my aunt, who was a very good friend of Mrs. Quentin's. Bryce is a couple of years older than I, I believe.'

'Gee, he's a good lookin' fella!' Cora said. 'I could really go for him! But he doesn't even know I exist.'

I smiled sympathetically at the girl and told her I understood Bryce was quite wrapped up in his manufacturing plant in Dayton. Then I mentioned that I had accidentally run into him as I was coming into Cincinnati and had had dinner with him.

'Lucky you!' the girl replied. 'Mmmmmm, boy! Would I ever . . . oh, my God, I'd better get back to the kitchen. Ellett will scream her head off at me.'

Cora scooted for the kitchen, and I picked up my notes and headed for the front stairs, since I wanted to keep out of Mrs. Ellett's way while she was preparing lunch. 'Discretion is the better part of valor,' in this case, I quoted to myself. I had decided that I would phone the garage on the library extension and would remain there until just before twelve-thirty.

Sam had carried my typewriter upstairs, for which I was very grateful. Not only did I need the machine, but also I was glad to have it out of the kitchen and away from the wrath of Mrs. Ellett. Like Cora, I too felt constrained to keep from incurring the unfriendly woman's displeasure.

A few minutes after noon I heard a car drive up the hill, and listened unashamedly to see if I could hear Bryce's voice. Apparently he had his own key, for I heard him come in the downstairs hall and walk through the back to the kitchen, where I heard him call, 'Hi, ladies! How are you?'

There was an answering murmur and a giggle from the kitchen, and I heard him say he'd try to find me. I thought I heard Cora's high voice, probably telling him I was in the library. In another instant he was there, and I was in his arms.

'Rosalie!' he cried, holding me tightly. 'You have no idea how anxious I was to see you again!'

In the circle of his arms I felt safe and secure. I wanted to believe he was my protector against evil, my knight to defend me against whoever it was that was seeking to destroy me. The tiny little bell that seemed to tinkle out a message of warning, to remind me to be on my guard, to not trust anyone implicitly—even Bryce—was stilled by the wild warmth of affection that swept over me. No, it was more than affection, my heart cried out silently. I had to acknowledge to my inner self that I had fallen in love. Totally. Completely. For a brief moment I thought of Kurt Richards, to whom I had given myself without restraint, thinking our love was so holy, so true, that our union was precious and a glowing fire. And my inner being rejected the idea that I could have thought I had ever loved Kurt! The feeling I had for Bryce was that of total belonging. For a second I allowed myself to melt against his body, and wondered how I could have ever in this world felt that Bryce might have been plotting to get rid of me.

'You're trembling,' he finally said. 'Have you been awfully frightened in this grim old house? I warned you things had changed, you know.'

'Oh, Bryce,' I cried, 'I'm so glad you're here! I'm really worried about your grandmother. I don't think she'll be with us much longer, and her poor mind—it's just as you said. She will be fine for a while, then it's gone. Do you know she thought I was Alice Roosevelt Longworth when I first got here? And besides that, the storm, and—' I stopped short, not wanting to tell him of my fearful apprehensions, because I didn't want to appear an utter fool if it actually was all in my imagination.

He pulled me down beside him on a leather sofa and comforted me. 'You poor kid! I wish I could have come right along with you yesterday morning. But I had to see Franklin in Indianapolis. Jobs for a lot of people depended on it. And I've got to go back to Dayton right after lunch.' He tipped my chin up toward his handsome face and said, 'Will you be sorry to see me go? I hope so, because I'll miss you, Rosalie!'

I felt myself blush, and wished it had been within my power to keep that flush of embarrassment from coloring my face and neck. Then I said, to cover my confusion, 'We'd better go down for lunch before the redoubtable Mrs. Ellett sends Cora upstairs after us.'

On the way down the stairs I told him about the sycamore falling against my car in back of the house, and mentioned that I had called the garage to come and get it. He said he had better pull around in back so the wrecker could get through the porte-cochere in case they came while we were having lunch. He ran out and moved his car and was back in short order.

'What a shame!' he said. 'And I'll bet anything they'll have to send to Cincinnati for a new windshield.'

'That's just what Sam Kuykendall said,' I told him. 'Certainly seems that it's just one thing after another.'

'Why, what else has happened?' He shot the question at me as we went into the dining room.

I couldn't bring myself to tell him about the scalding water incident and just merely murmured that I had been quite frightened, feeling as though someone were watching me

106

from outside the house. 'My imagination, I guess,' I said quickly, because I was sure that was what he would say. Then I told him how I pulled the drapery cord so fast at the dining room window that it had broken in my hand. He laughed, and said the cord was no doubt rotten, just like a lot of other things about the old house.

In a few minutes Aunt Francie and Miss Erikson came in through the hall, and the golden lights flickered in Aunt Francie's amber eyes as she greeted Bryce. 'I knew you were coming, before you called,' she said. 'Didn't I, Rosalie? Didn't I tell you?'

'Yes, you did,' I acknowledged.

Bryce laughed. 'Did you ever think about working with a crystal ball, Granny?'

'I wouldn't need a crystal ball, Bryce. I've always known these things. Sometimes I'm aware that unpleasant things are going to happen—not always—but for some reason or other I do always seem to know ahead of time about the good things.'

'You're amazing,' Bryce said, and helped her from her wheel chair to her place at the table. 'And besides that, you're pretty good-looking for a woman in her early sixties.'

'Now Bryce, you know I'm closer to ninety than I am to sixty.'

I glanced toward Miss Erikson and saw a dark look cross her face. 'Look at him buttering her up!' she seemed to think. The hateful expression in her eyes almost shouted the words! I glanced toward the kitchen and saw Mrs. Ellett coming in with a soup tureen, her grey hair pulled up into a tidy knot, her face wreathed in smiles. Quickly I flicked a brief look in Cora's direction and saw that she, too, was beaming. The nurse muttered something that sounded like '. . . too much excitement . . .', and it was easy to see she was irritated by the lighthearted banter between her patient and her patient's grandson.

Lunch was a pleasant interlude in spite of Miss Erikson's obvious displeasure at Bryce's sallies and Mrs. Quentin's happy response. We talked of our project, and Aunt Francie told Bryce how much we had managed to accomplish in a few hours' time during the morning. She asked him if he would be staying overnight, so she could have Cora prepare his regular room for him. He told her, as he had previously told me, that he had to return to Dayton. He had made a call at a factory close to Ripley where he had had to find out about some parts he needed for production at his plant, and thought he would just run in and see us for an hour or so while he was so close.

'I'm very glad you did, dear. And I rather think there are others who are pleased, too.'

Again that telltale blush stole over my face and neck, and again I wondered why on earth

I couldn't control it. Blondes and redheads blushed. Young innocent girls blushed. It amazed me that I, neither blonde, nor redhead, nor young, nor exactly innocent should be tortured so by something I couldn't restrain. I was as bad as Cora, I admitted to myself as I noticed her throw him a coy glance. Worse. I was supposed to be a bit more sophisticated, and I should have more sense than to wear my heart on my sleeve. Did I want to leave myself wide open for another crushing blow? The thought was sobering, but it didn't last. Every smile from Bryce brought an answering rush of joy from me.

Bryce left shortly after lunch, as he had said he must. Mrs. Quentin went up to her room to rest for a while, and asked me to come in about three o'clock. Since I had nothing else that demanded my immediate attention, I went up to the library to begin typing my notes.

The upstairs library, which adjoined the study of Aunt Francie's late husband, would have been a delight to anyone faintly interested in the art of seafaring. If I had been born a boy, and had been brought to La Colline to visit, I would no doubt have spent most of my time there.

In addition to the sets of encyclopedias, reference books, histories, and dictionaries, the library was replete with artifacts that had to do with everything related to sailing. There were nautical maps of the world, charts depicting correct methods of tying knots, paintings of clipper ships, a glass-enclosed cabinet that housed a magnificent collection of shells, and some of the most beautiful scrimshaw work I've ever seen.

It took me a little while to settle down to work, but once I got started at it, it went quickly. I suppose it was because I was deeply interested in it, and somehow felt an urgency to get everything on paper as fast as I could. When I glanced at my watch it was almost three o'clock. I looked up as Nurse Erikson came into the library and told me Mrs. Quentin would not be able to do any more work for the day.

'Is she ill? Or just confused?' I asked.

'Well,' the nurse said, 'she's too feeble to even sit up in bed. It's my belief that she shouldn't try to do any kind of taxing work at all. She's very weak, you know.'

'Yes, that's true,' I conceded. 'But she was in such good spirits at lunch! I know she had hoped to do a little work on the Glass Hat collection this afternoon.'

'I'm aware of that,' she said, and it appeared to me there was quite an edge to her voice, as if she thought I was questioning her decision. 'But I insist that she not be disturbed.'

I hesitated, feeling it was not really my

place to bring up the subject, but yet I was reluctant to sit idly by and let my aged friend simply slip away if anything could be done to help her. Finally I summoned all the courage I could command and said, 'Should we call Dr. Fentress, d'you suppose?'

Miss Erikson shook her head. 'I see no need for it,' she stated. 'She's sleeping now, and the doctor has said to let her sleep whenever she can.'

I accepted the nurse's decision, and said I would either be in the library or in the dining room, if she should need me. She assured me she would keep a close watch on her patient, and went back down the hall.

It was the first time since I'd been at La Colline that I had actively thought of Dr. Ivan Fentress, who had been Aunt Francie's personal physician as far back as I could remember.

'Aunt Francie, don't you think "Ivan" is a funny name?'

'No, dear. Not at all. "Ivan" means the same thing as "John," you know.'

'It does? Why didn't they just call him John, then?'

'Dr. Fentress' mother came from Russia. Ivan was her father's name, and that's what she named her baby boy.'

'What was HER name, Aunt Francie?'

'She was Marya Ivanovna. That means

literally, "Mary, daughter of Ivan." Now, if she had been a boy, she would have been Alexei or Georgei or Sergei or something IvanoVITCH.'

'How funny!'

'Not necessarily, dear. It's similar to the "Fitz" in Irish names or the "Mac" in Scottish. As a matter of fact, many languages designate the identity of the preceding generation. The prefix "Fitz" in an Irish name means "son of." For example, Fitzhugh means "son of Hugh." We have the same thing in the English language. A name such as Jacobson at one time was used to designate somebody who was a son of Jacob. So Ivanovitch could be loosely translated as—'

'I know! I know! Johnson!'

Again I was reminded of practical lessons I had learned from the elderly lady who always had time to answer my childish questions, who always explained in such a way that not only did I remember what she said, but also was spurred on to find out more about the subject at hand.

The rest of the afternoon dragged slowly by, for I was deeply concerned about Mrs Quentin's perilous state of health. My thoughts would dwell on the possibility of the elderly lady's slipping into a coma, then they would suddenly veer toward Bryce and the warm, heady feeling that seemed to sweep up from my very toes and wash over my body. I must have been in love with Bryce when I was a child, I decided. Possibly it was because of Kurt Richards' faint resemblance to Bryce that I had thought myself in love with him. But was it a one-sided thing? Was he just being charming, or was he trying to let me know, without making an actual commitment, that he, too, was caught up in what the textbooks usually refer to as 'a meaningful relationship?'

*   *   *

The dinner hour finally arrived, and Cora left for home. Miss Erikson said there was no change in Mrs. Quentin's condition. The doctor would call in the morning, and until he did there was nothing anyone could do. She was unable to talk to anyone.

'I think I'll stop in and see her for a minute,' I ventured. 'Just in case she happens to awaken and feel lonely.'

Miss Erikson pressed her lips together in a severe line, and appeared to be on the verge of telling me I must not disturb her patient, then relaxed her stern visage and agreed that it would be all right. 'But please don't stay too long,' she said. 'I don't want her over-taxed. There's a possibility she may rally from this siege of weakness. She has done so in the past.'

Mrs. Ellett grumpily agreed that this was true. I promised not to stay more than a few minutes, and excused myself from the table. After a little while I could see that she was sleeping quite peacefully and I dropped into the little chintz-covered rocker that stood near the window and gazed at the fragile figure on the bed.

Possibly five minutes passed, and since all seemed quiet and tranquil, I decided to go on to my room. Suddenly the frail body twisted and turned and with apparently no effort at all, Mrs. Quentin sat bolt upright in bed and looked directly at me. 'Be careful,' she said. That was all. And immediately she dropped to the pillow, closed her eyes and began to breathe heavily, deeply.

Very strangely, just at that moment I recalled the appearance of my apartment after Kurt had gone: the feeling that I had not left the furniture placed that way although I knew that no one else had rearranged it. Without even closing my eyes, I saw that the lineup of chairs, sofa, and tables suggested a tunnel, or a straight passageway drawing my attention to the door, while the words 'be careful' seemed to hang in the air. Involuntarily I shuddered. I tiptoed out and down the hall to the library, where I picked up a few books about the various forms of Art Glass and decided I would read for a while and then take a bath.

A TUB bath.

CHAPTER SEVEN

When I first heard the noise, it was in my dream. I had fallen into a troubled sleep and was dreaming that I was swimming. Which gave me a strange sensation even as I slept because I am one of those unfortunate people who can't swim a stroke. I was in a pool, swimming back and forth, very reluctant to touch any of the sides of the pool or even to grab hold of the ladder. But I was tiring and knew that sooner or later I was going to have to get out of the pool, or at least rest for a while before I could continue.

In the far distance I could hear a tiny 'bleep-bleep-bleep' and was positive that it was a warning signal of some sort that I must leave the pool immediately. The urgency of the signal awakened me, and for a moment I lay there drenched in cold sweat. My body felt as wet as though I actually had been in a swimming pool and I had suddenly climbed out, shivering with the cold.

Then I grew aware that the faint noise I had heard in the dream was an actuality. It seemed to be coming from the window; then it sounded farther away, possibly as though it were in the clothes closet. I lay there with the covers drawn around my trembling body and tried to convince myself that the noises were caused by normal expansion and contraction due to alternate heating and cooling of the pipes. But it sounded to my terrified ears very much like someone using a pry bar, quietly, stealthily. The faint 'bleeps' I was sure I had heard could very well be a squeal caused by the parting of window locks from the ancient wood of the frames. The longer I lay there, the more definitely I became convinced that someone was trying to break into the house. I certainly had no intentions of becoming the heroine who saved the place from robbery, and burrowed deeper into the mattress and the protecting covers.

Then the thought struck me that all that precious glass in the Victorian Pattern collection was eventually going to belong to me, and I suppose the idea that someone might be going to steal what was lawfully intended for my possession made me ease my reluctant body out of bed.

Throwing on my robe, I tiptoed to the door and opened it as quietly as possible. I felt my way down the hall and listened first at Mrs. Ellett's door, where steady snores and an occasional mumble of half-spoken words and phrases let me know she was sleeping soundly. Then I stopped at Aunt Francie's door, and at Nurse Erikson's door, and heard no kind of noise within either room. It was while I was standing with my ear practically glued to Miss Erikson's door that I heard the faint 'bleep-bleep' again. This time it seemed to be coming from downstairs, in the kitchen area.

I stood there, hesitating between trying to awaken the nurse or Mrs. Ellett and crawling back into bed. But in the back of my mind was the idea that many fires are set in the effort to cover up robberies, and I most assuredly did not intend to be trapped in a fire due to my own cowardice. The idea came to me that if someone were intent on stealing the glass collection, or the silver, or the valuable paintings, perhaps I could cause them to leave hurriedly if I turned on the kitchen light to indicate that occupants of the house were up and stirring around.

As I went down the back stairway, I couldn't hear any kind of noise at all. By the time I reached the kitchen, I had practically convinced myself I had imagined it. Since I was there, I decided to turn on the light and get a glass of milk out of the refrigerator. I switched on the overhead kitchen light, and at that moment heard the 'bleep-bleep-bleep-bleep' sound again. All thoughts of a glass of milk vanished.

Don't surprise a robber, you idiot, I thought to myself. A surprised burglar is going to be a nervous one. That's what the police are always stressing. A nervous robber will shoot first and then leave.

I forced myself to switch on the basement

light, feeling that if a burglar should happen to be in the cellar area the warning of the light flashing on might cause him to drop what he was doing and run.

'Mrs. Ellett?' I called with false courage. 'Are you downstairs?' I inched my way down the stairway, breathing in the cold, damp, musty smell that was the result of years of rotting wood, mouldy storage cabinets, and coal that remained in fine particles of dust and clung to crevices in the walls, even though the furnace system had been changed over to fuel oil many years ago. I could not hear the noise, nor could I hear or see the movement of so much as a mouse.

I stood there on the steps, not daring to descend any farther and almost afraid to even peer into the shadowy corners. For all the antique glass in the entire world I would not have opened the door that led into the laundry room, where the door hung slightly ajar.

The mere thought of the laundry room caused me to shudder, because it was in the laundry room that I had had the only unpleasant experience of my childhood as a visitor to La Colline.

It was in the spring, I recalled, and on a sunny Saturday my Aunt Caroline and I had spent the day helping Aunt Francie stretch lace curtains. Aunt Francie would never have thought of sending those curtains out to be laundered. They were far too valuable to risk mishandling by some careless person, so she always did them herself. She had been fretting because she had sprained her wrist and was unable to do the job alone, and Aunt Caroline had said she'd be glad to help her.

I had run down the stairs to get the curtain stretchers, which were wrapped in newspapers and tied around with string to hold them together. I had not turned on the light in the laundry room because there was enough light coming from the stairway for me to see the bundle of curtain stretchers just past the laundry tubs. I got the stretchers and started toward the door when the door blew shut in front of me. The grocery boy had opened the back door to bring in the Saturday order, and the draft down the stairway had caused the door to the laundry room to slam shut.

As I dropped the bundle I held in my hand, one of the needlesharp stretching points caught my leg just above the knee. I screamed with pain as well as fear and reached for the pull chain that activated the overhead light, for there was no wall switch there. Evidently I pulled too hard, for the chain broke off and what was left of it tangled itself around somewhere overhead. By that time I couldn't even remember where the door was in the inky blackness, and as I started in the direction of the door, feeling with my hand

119

for the knob, screaming all the while, my fingers came in contact with a spider web. When at last I did find the doorknob, I couldn't open the door. Spring rains had caused the wood to swell and the force of the draft through the house had made the door slam tightly against the frame.

It was scarcely more than a couple of minutes before Aunt Caroline and the grocery boy rushed down the stairs and the boy opened the door by the force of his brawny shoulder against it, but to me it was hours of agony.

Ever since that day the door to the laundry room had hung slightly ajar unless it had been closed tightly. As I stood on the basement steps, the horror of being locked inside that room, alone in total darkness, with blood running down my leg from the painful scratch washed over me afresh, and even though the pull chain had been replaced long ago, I could not bring myself to go in there and turn on the light.

Telling myself there was no point in standing there on the basement steps, shivering in my house slippers, I turned and started back up toward the kitchen.

The moment I had turned my back, I felt a slight rush of air that indicated movement of something behind me. Before I could even turn my head to see who or what it was, I crumpled to the steps in a blur of pain.

Someone had delivered a blow to the back of my head that brought me to my knees. I was conscious of the smashing blow, of the feel of the sharp corners of the basement steps as my knees were forced against them, of the smothering weight of a body that pinned me to the steps.

My last brief flash of thought was that I was glad I had taken a bath before going to bed. My dead body would be clean.

CHAPTER EIGHT

There was a strange, metallic taste in my mouth when I awakened. It was still dark, but I had the feeling that it must be early in the morning. I looked at my clock but my eyes didn't focus properly. The clock appeared to be surrounded by a layer of blanket fuzz. Finally I was able to make out the luminous hands pointing to twenty after six.

With a numb terror I recalled the attack on the stairway. Gingerly, I felt the back of my head. For some strange reason, there was not much of a lump. It felt as though it should have been the size of a lemon, at least, by the way it hurt. My knees ached. I ran an exploratory hand over the painful joints and found the skin intact. There were no deep

121

abrasions, as I had thought there would be. With every muscle and every nerve and every bone protesting, I tried to lift my head from the pillow. Wave after wave of nausea swept over me when I tried to rise, and I was forced to drop back on the bed.

My mind tried to assess what had happened, and refused. For several minutes I lay there trying to recall the dream I had had before the eerie noise awakened me. Right then it became perfectly clear to me that in my sleep, my subconscious had taken over to keep me aware of my dangerous position, and the aversion I had felt toward touching any side of the pool or the ladder indicated my deep distrust of all the occupants of La Colline. Except poor Aunt Francie, who I knew was slipping toward death, and the open-faced Cora who could not possibly harbor an evil thought.

Returning to my immediate situation, I knew I had been grabbed from the back. I had been slugged, either by a blackjack or a well-placed fist. I remembered my knees being in contact with the stairway as I was forced down and I remembered the intense pain at the back of my neck. And there I stopped. I could remember no more. How had I got back in bed? Had someone carried me there? Who? Why? Was there really a robber in the basement? Had he murdered everybody else in the house? Had I, somehow, managed to crawl back to my room after being left for dead on the basement stairs? A jumble of thoughts and half-thoughts tumbled and twisted through my mind as I tried to grope my way back to reality. Again I drifted back into sleep, only to awaken in what I felt was just a few minutes and struggle through the same thought patterns. As I lay there trying to swallow back the bitter bile that rose in my throat, a fleeting idea began to insinuate itself into my consciousness.

It was a nightmare. You only dreamed of going to the kitchen, turning on the light, going down the basement stairs and getting yourself slugged. Otherwise why wouldn't there be a big lump back there on your head, stupid? And why wouldn't your knees be scoured up? You probably twisted around in your sleep and pulled a muscle in the back of your neck. It's probably the cold, damp weather that has made your knees hurt.

By this time the idea had developed into a full blast of reason. After all, there I was in my own bed. My head hurt, my knees ached with a dull pain, and I was dreadfully nauseated. I told myself I was coming down with a virus. After all, what robber or murderer would carry me back to bed and tuck me in? Out of some smoky, dim recess of the past, I heard my Aunt Caroline say, 'Child, that imagination of yours just doesn't know when to quit!'

I forced myself to face facts. Before long, I had convinced myself that I probably had a touch of the flu or some virus infection and had struggled through a nightmare in my feverish state. That would account for my aches, that would account for my being still in my bed, that would even account for the repulsive, brassy taste in my mouth and the queasy feeling in my stomach.

Slowly and painfully I eased myself out of bed, stuck my feet in my slippers and tottered toward the bathroom. I splashed cold water on my face and wrists, hoping to alleviate what nausea that portended.

The murky fog that I had felt myself slipping in and out of had at last begun to clear away. I looked at the clock and saw that it was after seven. Mrs. Ellett should be in the kitchen by now, I believed. I went to the door, realized I was still in my bathrobe but decided that propriety could be damned, I didn't feel like dressing just then but I wanted a cup of tea and if Mrs. Ellett didn't like my coming to the kitchen in a bathrobe, she could lump it. Angrily I jerked at the doorknob, and found that the door was locked.

It was simply impossible for that door to be locked, I raged. I tried the door again, and it wouldn't budge. I rattled the knob, twisted it, pounded against it—all to no avail. I could not understand why anyone would want to lock me in my room, and I could not imagine who on earth would have done it. I screamed for Mrs. Ellett. I screamed for Miss Erikson.

'Mrs. Ellett!' I called, and the sound of my voice bounced and echoed in the room. 'Mrs. Ellett—lett—Miss Erikson—rikson—kson. Somebody—HELP ME!'

Nobody came. Weak from the effort of pounding and kicking against the unyielding door when I felt so miserable anyway, I half crawled, half dragged myself to the window. By this time I was whimpering with rage and frustration, and was determined to jump out the window even though it was at least a sixteen foot drop to the graveled parking area below. The memory of being shut up in the sooty black laundry room when I was a child that I had recalled sometime during the night, returned anew. Sweat drenched my armpits and ran down the small of my back. With trembling fingers I opened the oldfashioned window locks and using what felt like the last ounce of my waning strength, got my hands, then my arm, and finally my shoulder under the stuck window sash. The wood was old and the paint had peeled in many places, allowing dampness to penetrate into the fibers causing them to swell in spite of the storm windows. Oh—the storm windows! I hadn't even thought about them, and there they were, heavy and sturdy, and locked into place from the outside!

The tears could be held in check no longer. I sagged to the floor, shaking and crying. But not for long because suddenly the feeling of nausea could not be controlled any more and I had to make haste for the bathroom. Later, weak and totally spent, I lay back down on the bed for a few minutes.

I tried to think. To make some sort of plan. There was Sam Kuykendall—he would probably be coming around in an hour or so. Possibly I could attract his attention from my window, get him to unlock the door and get me out of this crazy place. Unless it was Sam who had locked me in in the first place. But if it had been a nightmare, if I simply had been feverish during the night and dreamed the whole thing, why would anybody want to lock me in my room? After resting for a few minutes, I began to feel strength returning and got out of bed for the second time.

With my hairbrush in my hand, I faced myself in the mirror of the dressing table. 'I don't believe you at all,' I whispered to my bedraggled reflection. 'It was not a nightmare. It really did happen, regardless of what you've been trying to tell yourself, and you've got to get yourself out of here regardless of Aunt Francie or Bryce or anybody else!'

It was a struggle, but I finally got into my sweater and slacks, spread up my bed, and stationed myself by the window, ready to pound on it with the hairbrush at the first appearance of human life below. Possibly five minutes went by, and it occurred to me that because the house was so old the lock on the door might not be tamper proof. I was sure I had read somewhere about burglars being able to unlock doors by working a thin piece of plastic down between the lock and the door facing. But, I asked myself, where in my bedroom or the attached bathroom would I be able to find a piece of plastic? I spent another four or five minutes searching fruitlessly for something to use for a burglary tool, while at the same time keeping an eye on the grounds below. It finally came to me that I had in my billfold a credit card sized plastic calendar, put out by a Berwyn building and loan company. Frantically I rummaged through the wallet and found the card I was looking for, ran to the door and found that it would fit in the tiny crack between the door and the frame! Something told me it might drop down further if I turned the knob as far as I could. I did so carefully, and the door opened without any help from the plastic calendar, which dropped to the floor.

My mind was suddenly so full of jumbled and contradictory thoughts that it truly began to frighten me. I had awakened at a stealthy noise. I had gone down the stairs and on down the basement stairs, where I was knocked in the head. Then somebody had carried me back up the stairs and put me in bed. Or was it just a touch of a virus and the whole thing was all a nightmare? I had been locked in my room. No, I had not been locked in my room, for the door opened as I gently and quietly turned the knob. With my stomach churning and my head spinning, I tried to convince myself that the door probably hadn't been locked at all. Because of the age and condition of the house, something had merely stuck in there and momentarily caused the door to jam.

Gathering all my courage, I tiptoed down the back stairs, not caring whether I startled Mrs. Ellett or if she heard me approaching her sanctum sanctorum. I knew I needed a cup of tea, and intended to lace it with a little brandy if possible. Pale sunshine, reflecting against what was left of the melting snow, poured through the east windows of the breakfast nook, which was slightly offset from the rest of the kitchen at the back. Mrs. Ellett was apparently nowhere around, although according to the kitchen clock it was after eight. The kitchen was strangely quiet. There were no breakfast preparations in progress, and not a soul was stirring. Oddly enough Cora was not there either, and she had mentioned to me that she was always at the house by around eight o'clock in the morning. My head ached frightfully and I was shaking with chills of nervous apprehension. Should I search the house to see what had happened to everybody? I asked myself the question and my feet wavered toward the doorway that led into the hall. Then I remembered how foolish I had been when I had cowered in the back hall after being so frightened by the feeling someone was watching me through the dining room window. Besides, common sense convinced me that I was too weak for anything except attending to my own needs. The first thing that I needed to do, I was sure was get myself that cup of tea.

A quick check around Mrs. Ellett's tidy kitchen showed me where the tea canister was, and knowing Mrs. Ellett, I was certain that tea would be in it. Smiling ruefully, I recalled what was in my own set of canisters back in the apartment in Berwyn which I desperately wished I had never left. Sunflower seeds for the birds were in the one marked Flour, paid utility bills in the one marked Sugar, scotch tape, mailing labels and twine in the one that was supposed to be used for Coffee, and untried but interesting recipes in the place where the tea should be. I put the kettle on the range, found the button that controlled the right front burner, got a tea bag out of the canister, and was trying to remember which cabinet held the cups when Cora came in.

'Hi,' she said, noncommittally, then turned around and gave me a searching look. 'Lord have mercy, Miss Bennett, what is wrong with you?'

'I don't really know, Cora,' I replied. 'I'm not feeling at all well, and came down to the kitchen to make myself a cup of tea. Do you know where Mrs. Ellett is?'

'No, I don't. That's where I've been, up to her room to see if she had overslept or something—which she never does do, of course—but when I came in a while ago she wasn't in the kitchen and I've been looking for her.'

Out of the corner of my eye I gave the girl a quick look, decided I could trust her as much as I could trust anyone else on the place, probably more than anyone else, with the exception of Aunt Francie, of course. I told her what I believed had happened because I could not trust my own halfhearted attempts at trying to convince myself it was all a nightmare and I hadn't even been locked in my room.

'Cora,' I began, 'last night I heard a strange noise in the vicinity of the kitchen or in the basement area below the kitchen, and came down to investigate. Mrs. Ellett was snoring and talking in her sleep, and all was quiet in Mrs. Quentin's room and Miss Erikson's room. I flipped on the basement light, I looked around but didn't see anything, then—just as I started back up the stairs—somebody clobbered me from behind. I was knocked out by a blow to the back of my head, and was apparently carried up the stairs and deposited in my own bed. I suppose somebody must have been hiding in the basement, possibly intent on robbery, saw the opportunity to knock me on the head, did so and then left.'

Cora's full pink lips formed an 'O' of amazement as she listened, then she interjected, 'But why ... why would somebody who had done anything like that ... anything that awful ... carry you upstairs and put you back in bed?'

'It doesn't make any sense to me, either,' I concurred. 'Of course it's possible that I managed to crawl up the stairs to my room and get into bed myself, but I don't recall it. I don't recall anything between the time that I felt the whack on the head and when I awakened around six this morning.' By this time I had found the bottle of Coronet VSQ and poured a healthy splash into my cup of tea. The scalding liquid worked wonders, and the cobwebs began to clear away from my brain. Thoughtfully, I stirred the tea and watched the spoon as it circled the cup. 'I wonder—' I began, and stopped, as the realization came to me that the whole thing followed the same pattern as the shower incident. There were times that I was positive

131

it was the nurse who had tried to scald me, then either in self-recrimination or because of her training in the alleviation of pain, had been constrained to ease the torture of the burns and take quite professional care of me. And now I had been attacked, and again care had been taken to partially relieve my pain. Could that brassy taste in my mouth have been the result of an injection of some kind of pain-killer? Could it have been Miss Erikson who slugged me?

'You wonder what?' Cora asked.

I had no intention of telling the girl what was on my mind, so I invented an ending to my unfinished sentence. 'I wonder if someone just wanted to be sure that I didn't see him—or her—leave the basement, but didn't want to really go so far as to kill me.'

Cora muttered, 'Well, now, it could have been! I tell you, I'm kinda scared, if you want to know the truth. Where do you reckon Mrs. Ellett is?'

I was examining the theory that Nurse Erikson certainly could have administered a knockout blow, and hardly heard Cora as she puttered around the kitchen, putting on a pot of coffee to perk. Big, strong, muscular, accustomed to lifting and moving heavy patients—it didn't take much study for me to come up with the answer that without a doubt the nurse could have been the one who had struck me with such brutal force and carried me up to my bed.

I'm sure I must have looked at Nurse Erikson through narrowed slits of eyes as she came into the kitchen. She hardly appeared to notice Cora, who was putting away the coffee canister. She glanced in my direction, flicked her eyes toward the clock and said, 'Uh . . . where's Mrs. Ellett?'

Cora answered. 'Nobody knows. I've looked all over the house for her and can't find her. Besides that, Miss Bennett was hit on the head by somebody or other last night. I don't know whether I want to stay around here and work or not. I'm thinking about going home. Too many strange things going on.'

Miss Erikson gave me a startled look then, and asked me what had happened. I repeated what I had said to Cora Geddie, and she said I had better have Dr. Fentress check me over when he came in. 'You appear to be all right,' she said after a moment. 'No dilation of the pupils or anything like that. But have him take a look at you. He'll be here this morning at nine. Mrs. Quentin seems to be worsening.'

Tears sprang to my eyes as I heard her ominous words.

'Oh, no!' Cora Geddie cried. 'Can't we get the doctor before nine o'clock?'

Miss Erikson shook her head. 'I called him once during the night last night,' she said,

133

'and he told me he would drop by this morning as early as he possibly could, which would be around nine o'clock. I was up practically all night with her. I tried to rouse Mrs. Ellett, and you, too, Miss Bennett, but nothing seemed to interfere with Mrs. Ellett's heavy sleep, as she kept right on snoring. I didn't get any kind of answer when I knocked on your door,' she said as she turned back to me, 'so I supposed you were sleeping deeply, too.'

'Well, I was,' I said rather shortly, 'but it wasn't exactly restful sleep after being conked on the back of the head. Didn't you hear strange noises downstairs while you were up with Aunt Francie?'

'No, I didn't hear a thing,' she said. Her words fairly dripped with acid as she went on, 'I was too concerned about my patient to be listening for burglars or bogeymen.'

'Miss Erikson,' I said, and I couldn't keep my voice from being sharp, 'I didn't imagine this blow on the back of my head, even though I did wake up in my own bed. I don't know who it was that did it, or why, but I know that someone did. And I also know that Mrs. Ellett is missing from the house, which seems very strange to me. I suggest that someone try to locate her, and believe that someone should call the police, too. I'm not entirely convinced that Mrs. Ellett had nothing to do with this business. After all, I heard these noises in the house, got up to investigate, got hit in the head for my trouble, then woke up feeling absolutely wretched. And now Mrs. Ellett is gone. For all I know, she might have been the person who knocked me out—I don't care if she was asleep when I first went down the stairs. She may have been the accomplice of someone who did. I don't know. I'm not making any accusations, but it does seem awfully odd to me that this thing happens and then suddenly one of the members of the household has disappeared. On the other side of the coin, Mrs. Ellett may have startled the intruder, or intruders, and may have been carried off and possibly come to harm. I'm going to call the police right now.'

My arrival at this quick decision startled me, for I normally tend to procrastinate and study things carefully before I act. It seemed to me that whether the cook had something to do with the attack on my person, or whether she was an innocent victim of the fiend who had slugged me, it was essential that she be located.

'Do as you see fit,' the nurse said in an offhand tone. 'I suppose that with Mrs. Quentin unable to conduct the affairs of the household and Mrs. Ellett somewhere away from the premises, you are as much in charge of things as anyone else. Except,' she emphasized with a sullen look, 'where my patient is concerned. In that area, I feel I still outrank you. Cora,' she then said, abruptly turning away from me, 'I wonder if you could fix a tray for Mrs. Quentin. I don't know whether she'll be able to eat anything or not, since she was so weak during the night, but I'd like to try to get her to take some nourishment.'

A flush of anger as well as embarrassment spread over my face and neck, but I marched up the stairs to the phone in the library intending to call the police. But I paused momentarily, even as I lifted the phone from its cradle, then replaced it. This is stupid, I thought. Mrs. Ellett must have relatives. Perhaps she's been called away by an accident or a serious illness in her family. I went back to the kitchen where Cora was preparing the breakfast tray for Mrs. Quentin in accordance with Miss Erikson's instructions, and asked her if she knew any of Mrs. Ellett's relatives.

'No, ma'am, I don't,' Cora replied sadly. 'She's a widow, is all I know. She never speaks of any children or grandchildren or anybody like that. And most grandmothers talk about their grandchildren if they've got any at all, don't you think?'

I had to agree. 'Did she live in North Rumford before she moved in with Mrs. Quentin?'

'Couldn't tell you that, either,' Cora answered. 'She was living here when I started to work, and that's three or four years ago. Why don't we go up to her room and see if we can find anything out?'

That seemed like a pretty good idea to me, and after Miss Erikson came and took the tray, Cora and I went up to Mrs. Ellett's room. There were no photographs around except one that appeared to be that of a congregation posing in front of a white frame church building. Small black letters in the lower right-hand corner identified the gathering as 'Homecoming, Mt. Zylpah, May 30, 1921.' We didn't see any kind of notebook or address book, and the only thing that appeared to be missing was Mrs. Ellett's tweed coat and big tapestry-covered purse that she always carried whenever she went away from the house, Cora told me, and added, 'which was rarely.'

While we were upstairs, I heard Dr. Fentress' car drive up. As we came down the back stairs, Miss Erikson came into the kitchen from the front hall with Mrs. Quentin's tray. The tray had not been touched.

Cora asked sadly, 'Wasn't she able to eat anything?'

'Not a thing,' the nurse replied. 'I believe I heard the doctor coming in the driveway.'

She turned and left the kitchen. Cora dejectedly said, 'I guess I'll have to fix something for lunch. Gee, I don't know much about cooking. All I do is the bedrooms and whatever cleaning Mrs. Ellett tells me. What'll I do?'

'You'll think of something, Cora,' I said with false enthusiasm, 'I'm sure. Right now, I'm going to get in touch with Bryce.'

I placed a call to the number Bryce had given me. There was no answer.

CHAPTER NINE

In pure despair, I went toward the door to Mrs. Quentin's room. Dr. Fentress was there with the nurse, and I wanted to see him before he left. Just as I reached the door, Miss Erikson came out, closed the door, and told me that the doctor had said Mrs. Quentin appeared to be sleeping.

I had wanted to leave.

I had meant to call a cab and go in to town, see if I could find a sleeping room somewhere until my car could be repaired.

I wanted to get out of La Colline, get away as far as possible from whatever unnamed danger it was that lurked there.

Now I couldn't. I had found it impossible to leave Aunt Francie when she was ill and feeble; it was more than impossible in the face of impending death.

138

'Do you know where Mrs. Quentin keeps her address book, or how to get in touch with any relatives?' Miss Erikson said.

'I've been trying to call Bryce,' I told her, 'but there's no answer at his apartment.'

'Well, how about his office?' she suggested, her voice heavy with accusation that I was stupid for not thinking of it.

I flushed and told her that he had mentioned to me that he didn't leave his apartment until about nine-thirty in the morning. Then I told her that Mrs. Quentin used to keep a small book in her rosewood desk. We both started back into Mrs. Quentin's bedroom, but the doctor stepped out into the hall just then.

'Dr. Fentress,' I said, 'I'm Rosalie Bennett. I used to live here in North Rumford. I don't suppose you remember me.'

'Oh, yes, I do, young lady,' he said. 'Remember you and all your family. I knew you were coming, Frances had told me. Can you get in touch with Bryce, do you think?'

'I've tried, Dr. Fentress, but there isn't any answer at the apartment where he lives. I believe Mrs. Quentin has an address book in her desk, and Miss Erikson has just suggested that I try to locate any other relatives. Miss Erikson tells me that there isn't much hope for Aunt Francie.'

'I'm afraid not, Rosalie. She's comatose

now. I'd get hold of that book, I think, and see if you can locate Bryce Willard and Charlie Quentin. There aren't any other relatives that I know of, unless it would be Bryce's father. Last I heard of him, he was in South America somewhere. But . . . well, do what you can.'

I suggested to Dr. Fentress that he come down to the kitchen for a cup of coffee. 'Cora has made a pot, and I expect you can use a cup. Miss Erikson tells me she had to call you during the night.' I said it because I wasn't at all sure she had spoken truthfully.

'Yes, that's true. She did. I don't know of anything that can be done for Frances, though. Now I know you're probably thinking of getting her into the hospital, and I am, too. But you see, Frances made me promise her a long time ago that when her time came, I must allow her to go in dignity and peace. She made me sign a statement in front of an attorney, and though there's some question about the legality of it, I want to do what Frances would want to have done. Even so, it puts me on a spot. You understand that, I'm sure.' He stared solemnly out the window for a second or two then went on. 'But I'm going to call and arrange for the ambulance to take her in to St. Joseph's.' He seemed quite agitated, and it occurred to me that probably Dr. Fentress had hoped all along that Aunt Francie would pass away suddenly and he

140

would not have to be torn as he was between his obligation to honor her wishes in the matter and his obligation to honor the Hippocratic Oath.

Miss Erikson walked with me to the rosewood desk, and I opened it. There was a tiny catch that released the drop front, and if a person weren't to know the proper spot to touch, it's almost impossible to get the thing open. The address book was where I thought I had remembered seeing it when Aunt Francie had directed me to open the desk and get a supply of notepaper and a pen. I took the book and told the nurse I'd start trying to locate people, and would send wires if I couldn't get in touch by telephone. She nodded curtly and said she would stay in the room with her patient. It broke my heart to think that Aunt Francie had just got a good start on the work that she so desperately wanted to do, and now the work would never be finished, unless by personnel of the various museums. And they would never in this world be able to save for posterity the personal anecdotes that Aunt Francie could tell about each piece!

I went downstairs and found Dr. Fentress in the hall, making arrangements with St. Joseph's Hospital for admittance of Mrs. Quentin as soon as the ambulance could get her there. He hung up the phone and told me he had called Vernie Apperson to send the ambulance, but it was out on a run into Cincinnati and would not be back until about noon.

I now had an opportunity to tell Dr. Fentress about my misadventure during the night, and to advise him that Mrs. Ellett was missing. But even as the words were forming themselves in my mind, I decided against telling the doctor exactly what had befallen me the night before. It could have been a feverish nightmare, I reminded myself as I recalled some exceptionally weird ones I have had over the years, and I could not bear the thought of appearing to be an utter fool. So I contented myself with merely asking Dr. Fentress if he knew whether or not Mrs. Ellett had relatives in the area, as she had left the house without telling anyone where she was going.

'I don't think she has any family at all,' Dr. Fentress stated. 'She moved in here with Frances after her husband died, about eight years or so ago, and I believe he was all she had in the world. No children, no brothers or sisters, or even cousins that she ever spoke of. Well, I'll tell you what. I'm going to stop in and make damn sure that ambulance has been scheduled to come up here after Frances just as soon as it gets back from the Cincinnati run, and then when I get back to my office I'll have Gracie check Mrs. Ellett's card and see if it shows the names and addresses of any relatives. I'll have her call you.'

'Gracie Claxton?' I said. 'Is she still with you?' The doctor smiled and said that she was, and he didn't know what he'd ever do without her. 'Well, ask her to let me know if she comes up with anything. Meanwhile, I'm sure I'll be able to locate Bryce before long.' I said it automatically, as most women will do when they think of the comfort of having a protecting male around the house: then I realized ruefully that perhaps I had more to fear from Bryce than anyone else. In addition, I realized that some stupid female type of reasoning made me want to protect Bryce in case he did happen to be involved. I wanted desperately to give way to tears. More than anything else, I wanted to run away from all this confusion and fear. But my Grandmother Bennett and my Aunt Caroline had instilled in me a sense of duty that I couldn't abandon. I felt that I had to at least try to get in touch with Bryce to let him know that his grandmother was fading fast. Personal integrity forced me to do what I could about trying to locate Charlie Quentin and Bryce's father.

The minute Dr. Fentress pulled away from the house and started down the long driveway, I wished I had never heard of the word 'integrity.' I should have just said, 'I'm going with you, Dr. Fentress,' I realized sadly.

Out loud I muttered, 'I hate people who complain about what they should have done.'

Charlie Quentin's latest address in Aunt Francie's book was in San Diego. I placed a call there and got no answer, so I sent a telegram. Hobart Willard's address was shown as in care of the U.S. Consulate in Caracas, Venezuela. I dispatched a wire to him, also. Then I tried to call Bryce again, at his apartment. There was still no answer. I called the office, and his secretary informed me that Mr. Willard had not yet come in for the day, and asked if I wished to leave a message. I told her why I was trying to get in touch with him. She was an intelligent girl, and sympathetic as well. She said she'd have him call me the moment he came in.

Returning to Aunt Francie's room, I found Nurse Erikson coming to meet me. 'I wonder,' she said, 'if I could ask you to do me a little favor.'

'Of course.'

'Well, I wonder if I could get you to stay with Mrs. Quentin while I run in to the laundry and pick up some clean uniforms? I'll not have an opportunity to do so later on, and I'll need to take some with me if I go in to the hospital with Mrs. Quentin.'

'I'd be glad to,' I replied automatically. There was nothing I could do for the dying woman, I knew, but since Miss Erikson had been up all night with her patient, I could at

144

least be of some help to her. She said she would be right back, and I assured her I didn't mind at all.

The room was quiet, too quiet. Through a glaze of tears I looked at the fragile head lying on the pillows. Then I walked to the south side of the room and looked out the windows, noticing that the sky had become partially overcast, and the very air in the room seemed to be damp with the promise of rain.

A sudden thought crossed my mind, and I went to the desk and got a piece of paper and a pen then went back and sat down by Aunt Francie's bedside. My thoughts at once shot back to the previous evening and Aunt Francie's warning, 'Be careful.' At the time, I shivered at the possible portent of her words, but had not really thought she was lucid because of the meaningless phrases she often spoke when she was 'wandering.' But now I believed she was absolutely aware of what she was saying: that she knew, even with her deteriorating mind, that I was in danger, and was trying to forewarn me!

As I sat there gravely considering this strange sixth sense of Aunt Francie's, I began to write down a set of numbers—(1), (2), and (3), then listed beside them those troublesome thoughts that kept battering away at me. Opposite (1) I jotted down *Who is in back of it?* It wasn't necessary for me to write any more than this. 'It' meant to me the strange feeling of being watched; the footprints in the snow; the unidentifiable noises I had heard in the night; the eerie feeling that somebody, for some reason, wanted me out of the house. Beside (2) I wrote: *Who whacked me on the head?*, and beside (3) *Why did he do it?* Then, very reluctantly, I set down (4): *Is Bryce to be trusted?* With pounding heart I wondered if he could have been the one who slugged me and then carried off Mrs. Ellett, who might have seen him do it. I answered the last part of that question myself. No. Mrs. Ellett was snoring and talking in her sleep as I listened outside her door.

One after another, I considered in the cold light of reason every person who had been on the premises. I examined minutely what motive any one of them would have had for trying to make me leave the place. I felt positive that someone did want me to leave, but not necessarily to kill me. But why? What evil machinations could be going on that required that I not be there? Who was afraid I would interfere with what plans? And why had Aunt Francie warned me to be careful?

As I sat there, trying to figure out what seemed to be a puzzle with no possible solution, believing somehow or other that only Aunt Francie knew the answers and she would tell me if she could, Cora came up to tell me that Dr. Fentress had called. He had stopped on the way down the hill to check on another patient and found it necessary to get her to Maysville at once. 'First he said he wanted to talk to Miss Erikson, then he said it didn't really matter, he just wanted to make sure she understood she was to go in the ambulance with Mrs. Quentin to the hospital, and to say that he would be there as soon as possible. But she's not here. Has she gone to the bathroom, do you s'pose?'

'No, she's run in to town to pick up some clean uniforms and should be back shortly.'

'Well, but—Miss Bennett, her car's still out there in the back.'

'In that case,' I said, 'possibly she did stop in the bathroom before she left. I'll tell her what Dr. Fentress said, but I know she's planning to go to the hospital, anyway. Don't worry about it.'

When fifteen minutes had passed and the car was still sitting there on the gravel apron, even I began to worry. First Mrs. Ellett had vanished, and now something seemed to have happened to Nurse Erikson!

'Did she go out through the back door, Cora?' I finally asked.

'No, ma'am, she didn't that I know of.'

I simply could not believe that the big rawboned nurse had disappeared into thin air. Of course she could have gone out the side door that led to the porte-cochere and Cora wouldn't have seen her, I reminded myself. But somehow it seemed that the time had

147

come for some kind of action, and without another moment's hesitation, I started to the hall to call the police.

Just as I heard the voice on the other end answer 'Police, Sergeant Browning,' I thought I heard the town fire siren blow. 'Yes, ma'am,' he said, and appeared to be writing down the information I gave him. 'We'll get someone out there just as soon as we can, Miss. Right now there's a three alarm fire raging down by the river, but we'll get right with you!' And he hung up quickly. By the way he spoke, I had him all figured out as a man who was doing his level best to soothe what appeared to him to be an overwrought, hysterical female. And then when I recalled exactly what I had told him, I could understand his reaction. After all, a cook had disappeared when she might have been on some legitimate errand, and a nurse was supposed to have left for town but her car was still parked in back of the house, and we hadn't even looked for her—for all we knew she could have fallen or passed out from lack of sleep.

'You know, Cora, we're really a couple of dumb ones,' I finally said exasperatedly. 'We haven't even looked around to see if Miss Erikson is still in the house. She could have fallen asleep on the john. I've known people to do it.'

Cora grinned sheepishly and agreed we

should give the place a thorough checking out. But a careful check showed that the nurse was nowhere around. Then I didn't feel quite so foolish about calling the police. The old eerie feeling of apprehension quickly replaced all other emotions.

I said I would go back up and look in on Aunt Francie, but before I could step away from the hall, the telephone began to ring. Hopefully, I hurried to answer. Surely it would be Bryce!

I said hello and waited for his vibrant voice to come over the wire. 'This is Mr. Willard's secretary,' is what I heard instead. In dismay I listened while she continued, 'I just found out that Mr. Willard called early this morning and told the only person who was in the office at that time, the cleaning lady, to get word to me that he was going out of town. Well, the cleaning lady forgot about it until just a few minutes ago, when she called me.'

'Oh.' My voice must have given away my total dejection, I was sure.

'I'm awfully sorry,' the secretary said. 'I've called all the places where he might possibly have gone—our subcontractors, any dealer outlets where there have been scheduling problems, the transportation companies we do business with—and have left word that if he should happen to come in, to have him call the office here or get in touch with you.'

'Well, thank you very much,' I said in a

small voice. 'I'm sure you've done everything you could possibly do.'

'I'll let you know immediately if I can contact him,' she said, 'and besides, he may be on his way to North Rumford now!'

'Yes, thank you ...' I replied, and with numb fingers replaced the phone in its cradle.

It was ten o'clock. It had been fifteen minutes since I called the police. Surely they could have sent someone up here by now, I muttered to myself. I walked to the north window and looked out. There was no indication that anybody was skulking about the premises. Not a shadow or a trace of a movement anywhere. Nothing but muddy gravel and a few patches of blackened snow that remained here and there. I paced the floor and finally sat down for a few seconds in a chair, wondering whether I should go into the library and phone the police again, or what I should do. For a little while I wavered between making another telephone call to the police station and calling a minister—the service station—the supermarket—anybody—to see if *someone* wouldn't come to at least give us a little moral support.

A gust of wind blew against the ancient panes of glass in the north windows, and with it came the rain squall that had been building since before nine. A cold, dreary rain. The final touch, I thought bitterly, to this siege of terror I had been living through for the past few days. A sudden peal of thunder shook the house, and I thought inanely of some kind of an old saying about 'thunder in January means . . .' but I couldn't remember the rest of it.

Then, just as suddenly as the thunder had rolled and shook the house, I said to myself: get out of here, Rosalie, while you're still on this side of sanity! Yes. That was it. I'd just pack up and leave. I'd call a cab to come and get me and take me to the bus station. I'd take the first bus out of town wherever it went! The police could find out what had happened to Miss Erikson. Aunt Francie would be taken to the hospital, and Cora could go home. After all, she did have a home to go to. And wherever Mrs. Ellett had taken flight, well, just let her be. I decided to get my typewriter out of the library and put it with my bags, and while I was there I'd call that cab. Integrity be damned.

The phone was dead as a doornail.

'Oh, blast!' I yelled in sheer frustration. 'This telephone doesn't work half the time!'

I lugged the typewriter into my bedroom and set it against the wall. Quickly, I began moving from the closet and dresser drawers all the belongings I had brought with me, methodically stuffing them into the two bags which I had placed on the bed. A thin glimmer of hope caused a flashback to a previous thought I had held, bounced against

151

my wall of frustration and presented itself to me vividly. Cora! Cora had a family, down the hill somewhere. I would ask her to go home, even though it would leave me alone with the dying woman in the upstairs bedroom. Surely there would be someone, her father, or a neighbor, perhaps, who might come up the hill and stay with us until the police came!

Back to the downstairs area I hurried, and found Cora staring at the refrigerator as if waiting for it to give her an idea as to what to do about lunch.

'Cora,' I said, 'our telephone is out of order again and I can't call out. Would you be willing to go home and see if your father or a neighbor could possibly come up here for a little while? It's beginning to look like the police are never going to get here, and I'm half out of my mind with worry!'

'Miss Bennett, my father's dead, and my mother works at the wool mill, so there's nobody at home. And the old man that's retired and lives next door, he's on crutches, and there's an old widow-woman that lives on the other side of us, and I don't reckon there's a single man on the rest of the street. They all go to work during the day.'

'But maybe you could telephone from your house—'

She shook her head dolefully. 'Whenever this phone here is out of commission, ours is, too. Ever' time it rains, seems like, up on the hill above town here, the phone goes out. I tell you the truth, though, I'm awful worried about Mrs. Ellett. Even if she is a sourfaced old hag, I still feel like something's happened to her. It's just not like her to go off the place! 'Specially without saying a word to anybody. She never leaves at all, exceptin' for to go to church. And you know, I've been turnin' it all over in my mind, wonderin' if she's gone batty over religion or something like that. Or if maybe whoever it was that slugged you has murdered her or carried her off.'

'I've thought about that, too,' I acknowledged. 'But Cora, she was sound asleep and snoring when I listened outside her room, just before I came downstairs last night. Apparently I'm the only one that heard the noise and I'm a very light sleeper. Miss Erikson said she didn't hear anything, and she was up several times during the night with Mrs. Quentin.' I hesitated for a bit and then said, 'I'm worried about her, too, Cora. I can't say I'm overly fond of her, but at the same time . . . you reckon she might have . . . gone out to her car and fallen asleep? We couldn't see her from the window if she had slumped over the wheel.'

'Let's go out and look,' Cora said.

I agreed, and we went out to the parking area but found no sign of the nurse. Cora kept up a running chatter that betrayed her nervousness and didn't do much for my worried state of mind.

I tried to put on a false air of normalcy. 'You know, Cora,' I said, 'much of our nervousness could be caused by very ordinary things. After all, we both know that Mrs. Quentin is in a coma and may not have much longer to live. And this is an old house, a weird and frightening one, made more so with the quiet of impending death pervading the atmosphere. And I could have imagined that somebody tried to scald me in the shower—as Mrs. Ellett said, the plumbing in this place is really atrocious. And Miss Erikson may have ... uh ... may have just walked away from here, as Mrs. Ellett has apparently done.' I concluded lamely.

I was whistling in the dark and I knew it. I think Cora knew it, too.

Pacing back and forth from kitchen to living room and looking for a patrol car that didn't come, I made up my mind that the only thing I could do would be to wait it out until the police came or the ambulance came, whichever was first, and tell them I simply had to get out of the place. Meanwhile, I would stay with Mrs. Quentin in case she should happen to rally from the coma. It would be unthinkable of me to just let her die alone.

Up the back stairway I went again,

wondering silently how many times I had been up and down the staircases that morning. I peeked into Edith Ellett's empty room as I passed, wishing that by some strange hocuspocus her angular frame would suddenly appear, sparse gray topknot and all. Idiot! I said to myself, and turned to go into Aunt Francie's room. My head bumped against the closed door, and immediately my whole body broke into goosebumps as I realized the door was locked and no one but that feeble, wasted, comatose body could have shut and locked the door! With a sob beginning to rise in my throat, I passed on down the hall to Miss Erikson's room at the head of the stairs. It, too, was locked.

For the space of a quick, indrawn breath, I wished fervently that I had never even thought about returning to La Colline. Then my breath came out in a scream.

'Cora! Cora!' I yelled, the words tearing themselves from my anguished throat. I flew down the front staircase to the hall below and almost fell as I reached the kitchen floor.

CHAPTER TEN

Cora, who had been standing at the sink uncertainly paring potatoes, came running toward me, drying her hands on her apron.

Her jaws worked, but no words came from her lips.

'Oh, Lord, Lord,' she finally choked out. 'What on earth has happened?'

'I don't know! Oh, Cora, I don't know! Aunt Francie's room is locked!'

'Locked?'

'Yes, and so is Miss Erikson's. Someone must have killed both of them, then gone down the elevator and out the side door, while we were looking at the car out there in back!'

Cora stood there with a horrified look on her face, wringing her hands as I went on, '... and we can't call anyone on this dead telephone—and the police haven't come as they said they would—I don't know what to do!'

People say that sometimes strength of character turns up where one least expects it. I was amazed when the girl suddenly drew herself up, clamped her jaws together for an instant, and said, 'I think Sam Kuykendall has a skeleton key. Let's lock every door in the house, make sure every window is locked, then search the house, both of us together, making sure nobody is in a closet or anything like that.'

'Not the basement,' I interrupted.

'No, we'll lock and bolt the door that leads to the basement, and wedge a chair under the lock. I don't want to go down there, either.

Then, after we're sure there's nobody in the house, I'll run down to Sam's trailer and get him to come on up here to be with you and keep something from happening to you. Then I'll walk on down the hill until I find somebody that can either drive me to the police station or get me to a phone that's in working order.'

I started to protest, partly out of fear for Cora's safety, partly out of my own terror at being left alone in the house. But I didn't know what else to do, and surely something had to be done. Then Cora pulled another surprise.

'Don't worry about me, none, Miss Bennett. There's a pistol in the pantry, been there ever since poor old Victor died, Mrs. Ellett says. I reckon it belonged to him, and I'll take it with me. It might be a surprise to you, but I'm a pretty fair shot with a pistol, and if somebody started after me, I wouldn't hesitate to pull the trigger.'

It was a surprise to me, and a greater surprise to find that the gun was right there in the pantry where Cora had said it would be. 'This here's a 1911 45-caliber automatic. A Colt. A World War I model. But old Victor took good care of it, just like he did everything else, Mrs. Ellett told me one time.' I looked on in awe as Cora checked to see if there was ammunition in it, nodded her head in satisfaction, and then we started methodically to make the rounds of the house. We began with the back door to the basement. It was already locked, and I wedged a chair under the doorknob as Cora had suggested for added protection.

As we approached the two locked bedrooms upstairs, I was tempted for a moment to suggest that Cora shoot the locks out. Then it occurred to me that that sort of thing was probably only done on cowboy shows on the late movie, and after all, it wouldn't be long until Sam Kuykendall would be there with a key. We checked every closet, every single place that could conceal so much as a three year old child, and then I let Cora out the back door and bolted it.

There was no denying the fact that I was frightened almost out of my wits, even though we had turned on every light in the house and pulled every drapery tightly. I paced from room to room, listening intently for the sound of an automobile in the driveway or any other indication that someone might be about—friend or foe. My heart yearned for the comfort of Bryce's arms. My mind told me to beware of Bryce. Beware of everybody, I told myself. Beware of everybody and pray that you'll get out of here alive!

Cora's words came back to me. 'My older brother showed me about guns. We used to go out and shoot targets before he got married and left Rumford. My mother liked to have had a fit every time we went out to shoot at tin cans and the like, but we had a lot of fun. You know those little milk cans? Well, he'd throw them up in the air and I'd knock 'em silly before they landed. With a pistol or a revolver, that is. He tried to get me to shoot his rifle or his shotgun, but heck, they had too much kick.'

'Does your brother live anywhere close?' I would have been most happy at the prospect of Cora's brother happening to drive in to see her.

'No, he lives in Oregon,' Cora said. 'He and his wife are in the potato business out there. I haven't seen him for three years.'

In the dining room I felt safer than any other place in the quiet, listening house. My eyes were drawn to the Pattern Glass shelves as I walked through the doorway, and more to keep my mind off my fears than anything else, I gazed at the graceful diamonds, squares, swirls, scrolls, prisms, panels, rosettes, fans, stars ... tracing with my eyes the identification of each piece. As I gazed at first one piece and then another, I happened to observe that one of the 'name' goblets was out of order. I didn't remember noticing it before when I had been looking at those goblets; it seemed to me that they had been arranged in perfect order on the shelves. The first thing that came to mind was that Aunt

Francie would have a fit. Those pieces of glass were always carefully arranged. I went to my room, got the keys out of my handbag and came back to the dining room and unlocked the cabinet. I picked up the offending piece and for a moment couldn't even remember the name of it. Oh, yes, I finally remembered, that's Carol. Not an old pattern, but rather a new one, I believed. Then I was ashamed of myself because I had forgotten that Aunt Caroline had given that piece to Aunt Francie because it was the closest thing to her own name. On the shelf below, another piece was out of line, standing in front of all the others. I couldn't recall the name of that piece at all. A rather stodgy thing, it seemed to me. Well, I thought, Aunt Francie must have been showing them to someone and failed to put them back properly. How unlike her! But then, I realized Aunt Francie had changed in many ways. I put the strange, rather plain looking compote back in line with the others. There was a faint circle, defined by the dust on the shelf, where it had formerly been placed. I locked the cabinet and thought about going upstairs to replace the keys, but decided I'd just drop them in the top of my bra for the time being.

A whiff of lavender hung in the air. There was no place for a breeze to come from, but I was sure I saw the drapery move. I jerked the drapery aside, not having the slightest idea what I'd do if someone was hiding there, but my grasping hands disclosed no one hiding there.

I went to the hall to check on the telephone. It was still dead. 'My God!' I muttered. 'I'm going to go stark raving mad if somebody doesn't get here soon.'

Again I went through the house, checking on each locked door and window, and on each side of the house pulled the draperies back only far enough that I could peek out.

'Peek out and see if there's a crowd, Rosalie.'

'No Serafina. YOU look. My grandmother would bust my butt if she knew I was peeking from behind the curtain.'

'Your grandmother would bust your butt if she knew you had SAID that, Rosie.'

We had giggled, Serafina and I, trying to sneak a look from behind the red velvet curtain that shielded us from the audience at the eighth grade commencement exercises. I dropped the drapery and giggled nervously in reflect. I had been able to see scudding clouds, wind whipped bushes, and an occasional sodden oak leaf beating futilely against a piece of gravel or a clump of brown weeds. Nothing else.

It felt like hours had passed, but when I

checked my watch I saw that it was only five minutes till eleven. I knew it would be utterly useless to try to read. My nerves seemed to shriek and I realized that every muscle in my body was held tight as a drawstring around a tobacco sack, as Sam Kuykendall used to say.

After another round through the house, for I was too scared to stay in one place for very long, I noticed for the first time that the drawing room door was also locked. But I could see through the glass that the elevator was on the first floor and empty.

I decided then that a glass of sherry might serve to relax me somewhat, and I certainly needed something to do the trick. Fear had clamped my teeth together tightly and I could feel great cords standing out in my neck. I remembered seeing a decanter of sherry and wine glasses on the glossy top of the buffet in the dining room, and headed back for what now seemed to me to be a veritable haven of refuge. As I passed the Pattern Glass cabinet, I flicked a look toward the shelves and simply could not believe what I saw.

I knew without a shadow of doubt that I had replaced the Carol pattern goblet and the compote that I couldn't identify. But there they were, out of place again! 'Carol' stood in front of all the other goblets, and the compote had, somehow or other returned to the front of the shelf it sat on. And in addition, I now noticed on the shelf above the goblets, a

162

spoonholder which I quickly identified as the Divided Heart pattern, standing in front of all the other spoonholders. Then once again I had that strange sensation that I had had in my apartment in Berwyn. I saw my furniture as it was after I had screamed and ordered Kurt out of my house, and in a flash of remembrance I saw it as it was later, all pieces aligned to draw my eyes to the door. Although I was aware of the significance of that thought-flash, my conscious mind did not want to admit it. *There is a connection. There is a message here, just as there was a message there.*

No, reason told me. Both things were pure coincidence.

But WHY did the thing keep hovering in the background? WHY did I feel as though I had my hand on the pullcord that would draw back the draperies, but was reluctant to apply the pressure that would let in the light?

By this time my teeth were actually chattering. I poured a glass of sherry and gulped it down, remembering no sooner than I had swallowed it that I had already downed about a tablespoonful of brandy with my tea. I figured it would probably make me ill, but I was in such a state of shock that I really didn't care. I knew I was almost incoherent as I began to alternately plead with the Lord to make someone hurry, hurry, hurry, and beg Him to give me strength.

163

Slowly I turned my eyes back to the Pattern Glass shelves, like a bird charmed by a snake, and with trembling fingers patted the key as it lay in my cleavage. The key was warm and damp with my nervous perspiration, but it definitely was *there*. I knew that I had the only keys that would unlock the cabinet, and I knew it was physically impossible for those pieces of glass to have propelled themselves forward to stand in front of all the others. And just as positively, I was sure no one else had been in that dining room while I was making another round of the house to check doors and windows and stopped to check the telephone in the hall. No one could possibly have slipped into the dining room, opened that cabinet, and pulled three pieces of glassware away from their accustomed places and up to the front of the shelves.

'I am not crazy. I am in complete possession of my faculties. My Social Security number is 35703 ... uh ... something or other.' I cried it aloud, then sat down and gave way to wracking sobs.

As if from a far distance, the meaning in back of all of it started to unfold. Haltingly I admitted to myself that there could only be one thing that was taking place here—and it had to be the result of a supernatural force. Immediately my teacher-of-little-children commonsense beliefs rebelled.

I don't believe in ghosts. I certainly don't believe in ... uh ... what do they call it ... apportation. There has to be an explanation. Some kind of an ultrasonic wave has dislodged those pieces of glass from their places. A far off explosion. A plane breaking the sound barrier. I don't believe it, I will not allow myself to believe it ...

But just as quickly as I had rebelled against the idea of some kind of psychic phenomenon being involved, my mind was forced to sweep rebellion aside and accept that fact which I did not want to believe.

It was clear as the crystal that sat on the shelves. Only one person would attempt to communicate with me through manipulation of the glass in that cabinet. Aunt Francie! And it had just as surely been Aunt Francie who had caused that furniture rearrangement thing in Berwyn. In some way or another, her extrasensory perception had caught my agitation and she had sent the message to me: HERE IS THE DOOR. BE READY TO LEAVE THIS PLACE. Then she had sent the letter that had brought me to La Colline.

Again I caught a breath of the fragrance of lavender, and it was apparent to me that Aunt Francie was trying to reach me in the one way she knew I would understand.

CHAPTER ELEVEN

Carol. Divided Heart. And a compote of some pattern or other. I pressed a hand to my throbbing temple, trying to figure the thing out. The Carol goblet was a gift from my Aunt Caroline. How, I asked myself, could my beloved aunt be involved in the mysterious message that I felt sure was coming from Aunt Francie? Aunt Francie, whose body was lying cold and dead in the locked upstairs bedroom! Divided Heart. That could be a reference to Cupid, I figured. Had Aunt Caroline played Cupid somewhere along the line? I racked my brain trying to remember what the other piece was, but its name escaped me completely.

There was only one thing I could do, and that was to go through the reference works on various patterns of glass and try to identify it. Without the name of the pattern in which the compote had been designed, there wasn't the least possibility of solving the riddle. My terror had left me when I made up my mind to accept the inevitable—that those pieces of glass *had* been moved by a ghostly hand—but I was still shaking with apprehension and anxiety. The reference books were in the upstairs library. I would simply have to disregard danger for a few minutes and round up those books, I realized. How I wished that the big library on the first floor had held encyclopedias and reference works! But nothing had ever reposed on the shelves of the downstairs library, which opened off the center hall at the far east side of the house, except beautifully bound classics. The downstairs library was for the convenience of guests, or for people who were looking for something to actually read. More than one crusty old man had brought his wife to a piano recital and sought refuge in the library until the event was over. I knew it would be useless to look for reference works in there. Not many people wanted to look up information while waiting for a recital to end. I remembered I had taken the books on Art Glass into my bedroom, but I knew all the other sources of information would be up in the library. With feet that were beginning to weary, I climbed the back staircase and hurried into the second floor library.

Senses sharpened by fear made me aware of the clinging odors of leather, furniture polish and wax, along with the faint smell of ashes around the little fireplace, although it was clean and gave no evidence of having had logs burned in it recently. It was probably the ash residue on the inside of the chimney that I could detect, I supposed. Then I caught the sweet, sharp fragrance of lavender and was aware without even thinking about it that

Aunt Francie had been in the room, probably not long ago.

As soon as I located the books I needed, I ran down to the dining room and leafed through them. Nothing seemed to resemble the design of the piece I couldn't identify. I studied every line drawing carefully and was about to give up in despair when I chanced upon a design that appeared to be what I was looking for. The cut of the base was the same, the standard was identical, the bowl appeared to be the pattern in question, but there was a figure of a bearded man on the knob that topped the cover of the compote shown. 'Bearded Man' was the name of the pattern, according to the book. Below the title 'Bearded Man' were the words: 'Some people call this pattern The Prophet or The Viking.' Well, I acknowledged thoughtfully, the piece I was questioning could be the Bearded Man—or The Prophet—or The Viking. It was supposed to be a covered compote, and without the cover, it lost its. identity. And even so, who was a Bearded Man? A Prophet? A Viking?

'... a name such as Jacobson at one time was used to designate somebody who was a son of Jacob...'

Thought-flashes began to bombard and penetrate my consciousness so fast that I could hardly keep up with them.

The Viking.

Eric the Red

Leif Eric*son*—Son of Eric

Ericson. Erikson.

Erikson is the Viking.

At about the same time I realized that Nurse Erikson was 'the Viking' about whom Aunt Francie was trying to tell me something, my mind raced back through time and I was a little girl telling Aunt Francie about my history lesson.

'Mr. Payton said that North and South Carolina were named in honor of King Charles of England.'

'That's right, Rosalie, they were.'

'But Carolina doesn't sound much like Charles to me.'

'There are many names that are what they call "variants" of Charles. There's the German Karl, the Spanish Carlos, the Rumanian Carol, all the feminine forms such as Caroline, Carla, Carlotta, Charlotte. Even Charlemagne means Charles the Great. Haven't they told you that in school?'

'No. They never tell us any good stuff. They just say "read it and learn it."'

I had to consider, then, that the 'Carol' goblet might refer to Bryce's cousin Charlie rather than my Aunt Caroline. And that blush

169

of embarrassment began to steal up from neck and shoulder and cause my cheeks to flame as I recalled Bryce's words, 'Charlie is gay.' Did Aunt Francie know? Was it with a ghostly tongue in ghostly cheek that she propelled that goblet to the front of the shelf for my attention?

So there they were, three clues to the mystery of La Colline.

The nurse, Charlie Quentin, and Cupid.

Or a heart divided.

Or a heart split in two.

Then I remembered ... and it took no more than a couple of minutes for me to race back up the stairs and find the list I had begun while sitting with Aunt Francie just before Miss Erikson disappeared, supposedly to drive to the village to get clean uniforms.

The first item I had listed was *Who is in back of it?*

The first piece of glass that I noticed was not where it was supposed to be was 'Carol.'

The second item I had listed was *Who whacked me on the head?*

The second out-of-place article that I had noticed was 'Viking.'

The third item on my list was *Why did he do it?*

The third article I had discovered where it did not belong was 'Divided Heart.'

Slowly the answer to the puzzle revealed itself to me, but still it made no sense. Charlie

Quentin was somehow or other in back of the fact that Nurse Erikson had slugged me, and the reason was love. But again I heard Bryce Willard's voice as he said, 'Charlie is gay.' And unless Bryce was lying about the whole matter, and Aunt Francie had been misled, too, something was off key somewhere. For certainly Charlie—wherever he was—would not be trying to get rid of me because he was in love with Leslie Erikson! No. That couldn't be it.

I tried another solution. Charlie and Leslie Erikson are connected in some way or another. Someone has tried to play Cupid and failed. No. That was worse.

I looked at my watch again and thought surely the hands must have stopped. It was just twenty after eleven. Again I tried to shuffle the pieces of the puzzle around until they made sense. My head was throbbing, and the glass of sherry seemed to be churning around in my stomach instead of helping to soothe my shattered nerves, just as I had suspected it would.

A tattered scrap of an algebraic equation floated through my memory and I found myself murmuring solemnly, 'If (a) plus (b) equals (c), then (b) plus (a) also equals (c).' Why the thing kept running through my mind I had no idea. It made about as much sense as Peter Piper Picked a Peck of Pickled Peppers. Yet, somehow I felt a subtle difference, a sense that it was most imperative for me to remember the phrase, so I said it aloud again. '(b) plus (a) also equals (c).'

While I was trying to read something into a hazy scrap of knowledge from years ago, I became aware of a kind of shuffling, scrabbling noise but I couldn't tell where it was coming from. It was not the 'bleep-bleep' thing I had heard before; it was definitely not as light as leaves brushing against the house or of mice clambering up hollow walls or across the eaves. The fact that I couldn't identify the sound made me even more anxious than I had been all along. I sprang to the window, threw caution to the wind and looked out. The sodden front lawn was just as quiet as ever. I dashed to every other window in the house and scanned the surroundings, but there was no visible activity anywhere.

I listened at the warm air registers for sound coming from the basement, but just as I crouched down, ear to the floor, the sound momentarily ceased. I ran to the telephone in the hall and lifted the receiver, ready to scream for help, but the phone was as dead as ever, and by that time I began to fear that the wires had been cut. I wished dreadfully that I had insisted hours ago that Cora Geddie go for help.

'Haven't you ever been afraid in this big old rambling place all by yourself, Aunt Francie?'

'What's there to fear, Rosalie? If thieves break in and steal, I'll feel badly about it, but then we're told in the Good Book: "Lay not up for yourselves treasures on earth," you know. So if my lovely possessions are stolen, I'll probably cry, but it wouldn't be the end of the world. I've tried to lay up for myself a few treasures in heaven, too, dear.'

'But ... supposing a robber comes in and kills you to get your jewelry and money and stuff?'

'I don't like to think of it, dear, but I've had a full life.'

How I wished I could remain as calm as Aunt Francie, even in the act of merely thinking about possible danger. I wanted to scream. I could feel the blood draining out of my face as I bit my lip to keep from it.

Then I heard a scream. For a minute, I thought it was I, in spite of myself, who cut loose with that spine-chilling sound. Then I heard it again, and realized with a leaden heart that it was not I. It was someone else. And that screaming was somewhere within the house.

CHAPTER TWELVE

My feet stood planted against the floor, unable to move under their own power. My mind gave the order to move, but somehow or other the order did not have any effect. I listened to the wild, high pitched, hysterical sound and tried to identify it, but other than being the scream of a woman, there was no way I could tell who was doing it. And other than the fact that it had surely come from somewhere in the house, I couldn't tell where it was, either.

A quick trip up the stairs assured me it was not coming from either of the locked bedrooms, where I was equally sure Aunt Francie and Leslie Erikson lay dead, murdered by a person or persons unknown. The sound seemed to be traveling through the furnace pipes or the cold air vents, yet it sounded farther away than the basement area beneath my feet.

It had to be either Mrs. Ellett or Cora, I figured. Mrs. Ellett, whom I suspected of being in some way connected with the murders of my friend and her nurse, as well as the abortive attempt on my life. Or Cora, who with the gun had gone in search of Sam Kuytkendall and had said she would go on to the police station to tell them we were not a bunch of hysterical women, the situation here was urgent. If it were Mrs. Ellett, I was almost afraid to go to her assistance. If, on the other hand, it were Cora, I felt sure I had nothing to fear and was anxious to hurry to her, to give whatever help I could.

'Oh, NO, NO, NO, NO!' came to my ears in a frantic wail. The voice sounded younger than Mrs. Ellett's this time because there were words being spoken; more than a shriek or a scream—not much more, but enough to carry a note of identification that it was a young voice, not an old one. I ran to the kitchen, positive that something terrible had happened to Cora.

Just as I entered the kitchen from the hallway, I saw the face of a man at the door that led to the outside. I heard myself blubbering disconnected sounds and thought sure my knees would buckle and I'd fall to the floor before I recognized the face as belonging to Sam Kuykendall. Quickly I ran to the door to let him in, and saw he was followed by a windblown and rain drenched Cora.

'Thank God you've come!' I sobbed. 'Besides the murders upstairs, there's someone screaming in the basement. I thought it was you, Cora, but you're here so it couldn't be—and it doesn't seem like the basement, either!' I knew I sounded confused, but the words came tumbling out

175

faster than I was able to control them, and in my fright I began to hiccup.

'Got here soon's as I could,' Sam said quietly. He listened for a moment, then said, 'That's the nurse, all right. She's prob'ly in the tunnel that connects the laundry room with the carriage house. I'll go down there. You stay here.' I noticed that he was carrying the pistol that Cora had taken with her. Cora was clutching her coat around her and shivering beside me, her face pale and her hands clenching themselves together.

'The tunnel?' I said, but no one answered me. Sam had already started down the basement stairs. I looked at Cora, wondering if she knew what he meant.

'No, ma'am,' she said as she read my inquiring, open-mouthed gaze. 'I don't know anything about any tunnel. But the police are on their way. And the telephone's not just out of order on account of the weather, the wires have been cut. I saw that when I went out the back door toward Sam's. Whee-ew! I ran all the way down there and hailed Betty Mae Crosby at the foot of the hill—that is, after I found Mrs. Ellett a-layin' on the ground with a busted ankle—and Betty Mae, she said she'd call the police. Great God Almighty! What's goin' on here, anyway?'

'After ... after you found Mrs. Ellett? Where was she?'

'Just this side of Sam's trailer, Lord love

176

her. Well, not just this side, I mean fairly close, though. I'll tell you all about it soon as I catch my breath. You said you thought it was me a-hollerin' as we came in? I heard somebody screamin' too, and I figured it was you! We got here just as fast as we could!'

'It wasn't my screams that you heard. Evidently it's Leslie Erikson, and somebody's with her, and I'm so afraid it's—No! It can't be.'

I clenched my fists so hard that my fingernails dug into my palms. Almost afraid to even think it for fear it would lend strength to the horrid idea, I admitted to myself that Bryce had to be the other person in the basement with Nurse Erikson. In the tunnel, that is. Wherever the tunnel was. As though the picture were propped up in front of me, I could see in my mind's eye the arrangement of the Pattern Glass in the cabinet: Carol. Viking. Divided Heart. Charlie Quentin had sent Leslie Erikson to get rid of Aunt Francie. I came along so he tried to kill me, too. But then she fell in love with Bryce. All that stuff she had said about Bryce was just to throw me off. That had to be what the Divided Heart was for. But Bryce found out about it and was down there bent on murdering her ... No, that was silly, I told myself. But—I had not been able to reach Bryce on the phone. He had merely called in to his office and said he'd be out of town.

'Out of town' could most certainly be North Rumford, where he could easily be in that tunnel under his grandmother's house trying to kill Leslie Erikson. Unless Sam got there first.

But why had Mrs. Ellett run out in the rainy dawn toward Sam Kuykendall's trailer?

With a dry throat, and hoping against hope that Bryce was in no way involved in this miserable mess, I said to Cora, 'Well, there's only one way to find out who ... who's down there. I'm going down, I don't care what Sam said.'

In the distance I could hear the faint sound of the police siren, now farther, now nearer as the car sped up through the winding driveway toward the top of the hill. Cora volunteered to stay and dispatch someone down to Sam's trailer, where she and Sam had carried Mrs. Ellett and left her.

I crept down the basement steps and into the laundry room where I had been too terrified to enter the night before. Sam had pulled the cord that illuminated the ceiling fixture, and I stared in amazement as he pushed against the concrete block wall with his shoulder and a whole section of the wall pivoted and turned to reveal steps that led to a brick-walled tunnel.

The hysterical screams grew louder, and only a few feet inside the underground passageway I could see the shadowy form of

Leslie Erikson reflected in the glow of a huge flashlight. She was bent over the crumpled body of a man, wailing, screaming, sobbing, and occasionally shaking the man by the shoulders.

'Charlie, Charlie!' she screamed, then ran her hands through her wild, disheveled hair and moaned.

'Charlie Quentin?' I whispered at Sam's back.

'Looks like him, near as I can remember,' Sam replied, softly. Haven't seen him in a coon's age.'

It was surprising to me that Sam could move as fast as he did, with his stiff left leg. But in one lithe movement, he sprang forward and grabbed Leslie Erikson and pulled her away from the blond young man, who looked very dead.

Under his strong arms that pinned her down, she threshed from side to side and screamed, 'He can't be! The whole thing was his idea, and now he's died and left me with it!'

'Hush!' Sam ordered, trying to calm the anguished nurse.

'But it's true,' she continued to wail. 'He knew Mrs. Quentin wasn't going to leave him a thing in her will, everything's going to go to Bryce, the damn brown-noser, he was always buttering her up and she thought the sun rose and set in his rear end, so Charlie got me to

179

come here and I was supposed to give the old lady sterile water instead of insulin and get her out of the way while he found the box of money old Victor had stashed away somewhere or other. But I just couldn't do it, 'cause she was going to die anyway. And then that mealy-mouthed Bennett girl showed up and Charlie and I couldn't work in the tunnel because she kept sticking her nose into things, and Charlie made me clobber her and wanted me to give her an overdose of Nembutal but I just gave her enough to knock her out until after eleven o'clock when we were supposed to split out of here and we were going to get married!' When she saw me hovering in back of Sam she started waving her arms around again and screeched at me, 'Why the hell didn't you SLEEP? You just made everything so complicated ... And now he's dead, and everything's ruined!'

So Charlie was in back of it. And Erikson, the Viking, had been the one who had slugged me. And suddenly the scrap of the algebraic equation came back to me and I said aloud, hardly aware that I was speaking, 'Oh. Yes. (b) plus (a) *also* equals (c).'

Sam Kuykendall turned around as if he had just then realized I was standing there, and asked me what the hell I was doing there anyway when he'd told me to stay upstairs.

'It's all right, Sam,' I said. Erikson was in love with Charlie. It wasn't Charlie being in

180

love with Erikson at all, and Bryce had not lied to me. Bryce hadn't even entered into it. But before I could do any more toward putting the pieces of the puzzle together, the police had arrived and an arresting officer busily set about reading Leslie Erikson from his little book that she had the right to remain silent, the right to counsel, and so on.

CHAPTER THIRTEEN

The police took Leslie Erikson away, on a preliminary charge of being an accessory before the fact of robbery. Shortly after that, a squad of four stout men carried Mrs. Ellett up to the house on a stretcher to await Dr. Fentress' ministrations to her sprained ankle. Sam Kuykendall opened Aunt Francie's door with his skeleton key and came out sorrowfully shaking he head.

'She's gone,' he said. 'We'll need Dr. Fentress to pronounce her dead before she can be taken to Apperson's. And guess we'd better leave Charlie there in the tunnel until Fentress comes, too.'

Sergeant Mathews, who had apologized profusely because they could not get to the house before they did, said he would send the doctor so he could take care of Mrs. Ellett's ankle while he was at the house, and would also dispatch a telephone repairman to get our phone back into service immediately. Cora flew back to the kitchen to make a huge pot of coffee while I went to the side door to await the doctor.

While I was standing there, tears streaming down my cheeks, I thought I heard the muffled sound of a car grinding up the hill. Must be my head roaring, I thought. It couldn't be Dr. Fentress already. I closed my eyes and pressed my hands against my forehead, trying to think, to plan, to figure how soon I could get out of this madhouse of violence, decay and death. A big brown station wagon pulled into the driveway. It was Bryce.

He lost no time in getting out of the car and running toward the house, and when he saw me standing there, he ran to me and gathered me protectively in his arms. 'Rosalie, darling! Are you all right? I met police cars coming down the hill and was so afraid...'

'I'm all right, Bryce. Oh, I'm fine now that you're here! But you'll never believe all that has—' I stopped abruptly, lifted my head from his shoulder and looked him straight in the eye. 'I've been trying to get hold of you since early morning. How did you happen to come? Did you get in touch with your secretary?'

'No, I didn't. I got a call from up near Columbus last night. A fellow wanted me to

182

call on him first thing in the morning about a new dealer outlet, and I left word at the plant and took off early. But a strange thing happened—I was driving along the expressway just beyond Springfield when something seemed to literally pull me off the road at the next exit. I sort of had a feeling something must be wrong, and decided I'd have a cigarette. Well, when I lit the thing and started to take a drag of smoke, it tasted just like perfume smells. Yeeeeech.'

'Lavender,' I said in a knowing tone.

'Lavender?' he repeated. 'Oh, you mean lavender perfume.'

'Yes. Aunt Francie's perfume.'

'God!' he exclaimed. 'This is really weird! Well, I turned south and headed straight for North Rumford, stopping only long enough to get gas and to try to reach you by phone. But every time I called, I'd get a busy signal. What has happened, Rosalie? Is it Grandmother?'

I nodded mutely, then when I felt I could control my voice I told him what I knew, which was pretty meager information. By the time I got to the episode in the tunnel, with the crazy rantings of the nurse, Dr. Fentress had arrived. We went with him to the upstairs bedroom where Aunt Francie lay, the gray mask of death upon her face. Bryce's hand clung to mine. 'Oh Granny!' he cried. 'How I wish I had got here sooner!'

183

'You did all you could for her Bryce. Your visits meant a lot to her,' said the doctor. 'She often told me that you brought more sunshine into her life than any other living soul. Well, poor old girl! At least she was allowed to die in dignity, without a bunch of obscene hospital machinery sustaining existence when it was time for her to go. You say Charlie Quentin's in the basement?'

Bryce accompanied the doctor down to the tunnel and I collapsed in a chair at the kitchen table.

'It's Charlie Quentin, all right,' Dr. Fentress said on his return. 'Apparently a coronary. In view of the odd circumstances, the coroner will have to make a report, though. But I'll tell Vernie Apperson to come after him and poor old Frances, too. The coroner can do his thing at the funeral home.'

Bryce seemed to be in almost as much of a daze as I was. I knew that he and his cousin had never been at all close, could even remember the squabbles they were always getting into when we were all young kids, but nevertheless it was bound to be a shock to him, I knew. Especially since he had lost his grandmother at the same time, and he really did love his grandmother. Bryce had my sympathy, for I was as fond of my grandmother as he was of his, and neither of us had had the normal care of a mother. Bryce because his mother had committed suicide; I because my mother was never at home.

'Now let's see about Edith Ellett's ankle,' the doctor said after a moment. 'Where've you put her?'

'She's on the couch in the sun parlor,' I volunteered, and Bryce and I went with him to the sunny room on the southeast side of the house. 'She seems to be in pretty good shape, Cora tells me, except for the ankle, especially considering her age and the fact that she was lying on the ground in the rain for over four hours.'

'How'd she happen to sprain the ankle, Rosalie?' the doctor asked. 'And why was she out in the rain all that time? Didn't she holler? Didn't anybody hear her?'

'I don't know anything about that part of the story,' I admitted, 'except for the fact that Cora found her when she went to get Sam. You know this morning I called the police and then I felt so foolish because she could have just gone out on an errand, then there was the fire on the riverfront and they didn't come ... Oh, Dr. Fentress, after you had left I wished and wished I had just left with you! I've been frightened half to death.'

Bryce wanted to know what I was talking about, and I told him, then mentioned that Cora had said she'd tell me how Mrs. Ellett was involved, but that things had just been happening too fast.

185

By this time we had reached the sun parlor and found Mrs. Ellett gritting her teeth together in pain. Dr. Fentress suggested soaking the injured ankle in a foot tub of warm water, and I went in search of Cora to ask her where I could find one. When I returned, I heard him tell her it didn't appear that any ligaments were torn, and then he asked her if she felt all right otherwise.

'Yes, I'm all right,' she said, 'but no thanks to that dam-fool Sam. He had that radio of his'n a-goin' so loud he couldn't hear me hollerin' for him, and him not more'n fifty feet away.'

'What were you doing out there in the rain, anyway?' the crusty old doctor asked as he lit his pipe.

'Why, dang it, I heard some kind of a queer noise somewhere in the house and went downstairs to investigate it. I slipped out the side door and walked around to the back and peeked in the cellar windows to see what I could see. Well, I couldn't see very much, but there was an occasional flicker of light here and there, and then one time I saw the cellar light go on and heard some kind of a commotion, 'n' then I saw the light go on in Miss Bennett's bedroom. Well, I figured she was up to some kind of shenanigans, and decided the thing to do would be to lock her up in her room and go for help. That-a-way, see, if she was mixed up in somethin' she oughtn't to of been, it would keep her from gettin' out, 'n' then on t'other hand, if someone was after her for some reason or other, they couldn't get to her! So I sneaked back up the stairs and locked her in. I reckon this was about five-thirty or so. Then I went back down stairs and was a-goin' to call the police on the phone in the hall, but out the back window I thought I saw the shadow of a man sneakin' from the carriage house to the outside basement entry. So I locked the kitchen door that goes to the basement, and when ever'thing was quiet in the house, I took off down through the trees toward Sam's. But before I got to his trailer, I stepped in this dang gopher hole and it threw me to the ground. I hollered and hollered, but like I say, he had his head in that dang radio and didn't hear me.'

Cora had told me she would bring the tub of hot water into the sun parlor, and Dr. Fentress thanked her as she came in and eased the older woman's discolored foot into the warm bath. 'Now, I want you to soak that for fifteen minutes or so, then we'll get a bandage on it and you can get around in the wheel chair for a couple of days. Give it a hot soak every once in a while and chances are it'll heal up all right.'

Something was bothering me, but I didn't know quite how to put it in words. While I was pondering how I could say what I had on

187

my mind, Bryce said it for me.

'Mrs. Ellett, didn't it worry you at all to know you were leaving three women in the house with a possible murderer?'

'Well, no, it didn't. Not at first, anyway, because like I said, I locked the door from the kitchen to the basement and I had already locked Miss Bennett in her room. And I've been around too many dyin' people not to know that Miz Quentin was not long for this here earth, and that Leslie Erikson I never did like and didn't care much what happened to her. But then I got to thinkin' about that lock on Miss Bennett's room. It don't work too well, somehow or other. Thing is, if you twist the knob just right the plunger falls out of place. And that did worry me some. But on t'other hand, if a fella didn't know that you have to turn the knob real easy-like to make that plunger fall out, no one could ever have got that door unlocked.' She gave me a sidelong glance. 'How did you get out, anyway?'

'I found the secret, Mrs. Ellett. Purely by accident.'

'It's sure a Lord's wonder. Well, I want to tell you I was mighty glad to see Cora Geddie comin' down the path! See, I figured I'd be back at the house with Sam before Cora got to work. I really did worry about what might a-happened to her!'

*   *   *

Edith Ellett hopped into the kitchen between Bryce and Dr. Fentress. She flatly refused to use the wheel chair Aunt Francie had moved about in, saying she would much prefer a pair of crutches. Dr. Fentress gulped a cup of coffee and left, saying he would stop in at Apperson's Mortuary on the way since the phone repairman had not yet come to patch up the severed wires.

Bryce recalled that the doctor had mentioned something about stopping in at Apperson's while we were in the kitchen, but said that at the time he had been so stunned by the course of events that he had hardly realized what was said. 'I'll go see Vernie Apperson myself, Dr. Fentress,' he said. 'After all I'm, apparently all that's left of the family and it's my responsibility to see that arrangements are made. And from there, I'll go to police headquarters to see what I can find out.'

By the time he returned, the telephone repairman had come and gone, and Cora and I, under Mrs. Ellett's supervision, had managed to prepare lunch.

'Well, people,' Bryce said as he came into the kitchen, 'Leslie Erikson has given a statement that is really weird.'

'Weird or not,' Sam Kuykendall said, 'I'd sure like to know what she said.'

189

'Well, here it is: Leslie Erikson met Charlie in a bar in Kansas City. She fell hard for him, and when he told her about a plan he had to recover a fortune in hidden money, she agreed to do what he suggested. Charlie knew that Grandmother was ill, although it had been several years since he had been here, but he got Erikson to come and take care of Grandmother saying that her salary was being paid by her grandson. Grandmother was pretty confused when Erikson first came, and when she mentioned to me that she wasn't going to allow me to pay the nurse's salary any more, I just assumed it was because her mind was not quite what it should have been and didn't argue with her. Incidentally, Erikson made out pretty well, because I paid her salary and Granny did too! Anyway, according to Erikson's statement, Charlie talked her into coming here, and she was to gradually withdraw the insulin from Grandmother, substituting sterile water for insulin in the injections. But Erikson insists she didn't do it, because she knew Grandmother was fast slipping away. Every night though, Erikson gave Grandmother some medication to make her sleep, and with Mrs. Ellett being such a sound sleeper, Erikson and Cousin Charlie could search the carriage house, where Charlie was sleeping, by the way, and the tunnel and the basement for the metal box Charlie was sure Victor had stashed away somewhere. You see, Charlie remembered that Victor had this metal box years ago but it was gone when Victor died. Everybody else assumed that Victor had simply thrown away the old box, or gotten rid of it in some manner or another, but Charlie was sure it was around the place somewhere. So he used a metal detector to—'

'A metal detector!' I burst in. 'That's what the noise was!'

'When you woke up and went downstairs to investigate?' Bryce asked. I nodded and he continued. 'Yes. Well, they had found the box all right—'

'In the tunnel?' Sam asked.

'In the tunnel,' Bryce said. 'And it's funny. I remember talking to Charlie once about the possibility of old Victor having money stashed away somewhere because when he died there wasn't more than a few dollars in his room in the carriage house, and he had no family and no money in the bank. Grandmother paid the expenses of his burial; there were no funds found any place. So it was logical to assume he must have done something with the earnings he accumulated over the years. Victor didn't drink or gamble, and no one ever heard of his being a ladies' man...

'Well, we were kids—I was seventeen and Charlie was fifteen—and I forgot about it completely, but evidently Charlie never got it out of his mind. Then when you turned on

191

the basement light, Rosalie, and called down the stairway to see if it were Mrs. Ellett, Charlie and the nurse jumped into the laundry room and turned off their flashlights. And when you started back up the stairs, and had your back turned to the door into the laundry room, the nurse made a flying tackle and gave you a rabbit punch on the back of the head. While you were out, she and Charlie carried you upstairs and put you in your bed.

'Charlie ordered the nurse to finish you off with an injection of Nembutal, and leave a bottle with two or three sleeping pills in it alongside your bed, to make it appear that you had taken an overdose; then they were to get on with the search for the hidden money. But Erikson said she didn't do what Charlie told her because although, in her words, you were snooping around, she couldn't force herself to do you in, anymore than she could murder my Grandmother. Instead, she gave you a shot of Codeine that should have kept you sleeping until past eleven in the morning, by which time she figured Grandmother would be gone, and they would load the box into the Erikson car and take off. They had the whole thing planned down to the last detail. Leslie was to go to bed and sleep until seven-thirty, then take a tray to Grandmother and wait for the doctor whom she had called at five in the morning to get there at nine. She was then to manufacture an excuse to go after clean uniforms, leaving Mrs. Ellett with Grandmother. Instead, she planned to be picking up Charlie who would have hidden himself in her car. Charlie would be wearing women's clothes and she would drop him at the bus station, then she would meet the bus in Cincinnati and the two of them would be on their way west with Victor's money. Plus whatever stolen jewelry and art objects she could manage to get away with.

'But things didn't work out the way they had planned them. You, Rosalie, woke up long before the time the nurse had anticipated. And Mrs. Ellett had disappeared. Improvising, Leslie carried out what she could of the plan, and even palmed a set of keys while you were looking for the address book, hoping one of them would unlock the unwieldy metal box. When she left you with Granny, ostensibly to go after clean uniforms so she would have a supply to take with her to the hospital, she actually slipped out the side entrance and cut the phone wires—'

'Right after your secretary called, Bryce,' I cut in. 'No wonder the phone was dead just a few minutes later.'

'It sure was,' Bryce continued. 'Then she waited till the coast was clear and went up and filled a suitcase with jewelry, Boehm birds, Bing & Grondahl Christmas Plates, anything small but valuable that she thought she could get away with, then locked her room and Grandmother's to allow additional time before the theft of the valuables would be discovered, came back downstairs in the elevator and locked the door of the room that gives entry to the elevator by snapping the plunger lock. She hurried out the side entrance and around to the car in back, where, according to plan, Charlie would be hidden.

'But Charlie wasn't there.

'She figured he was having trouble getting the heavy box out of the niche in the ceiling of the tunnel where Victor had cached it. Since she had what she was pretty sure was the key for it, she went to the outside entrance to the basement, slipped into the laundry room and from there into the tunnel, looking for him, expecting to merely un*lock* the box, scoop out the cash, and split.

'When Sam found her, she had the bunch of keys in her hand. The only thing that didn't work out was the final phase of the caper—and Charlie's coronary took care of that.'

He hesitated for a moment and then said, 'Knowing Charlie, I'm sure he wouldn't have married the girl anyway. She was just a means to an end. And Charlie did have a lot of charm that he could turn on if he thought it would pay.'

'Well, for ever more!' Mrs. Ellett

exclaimed. 'Now how do you reckon Miz Quentin came to have the key for Victor's box?'

Bryce shrugged. 'Lord knows. Maybe he asked her to keep it for him, intending to tell her the money he had saved was to pay for his burial, and then died before he could tell her.'

'Well, one thing I'd like to know,' I said very thoughtfully. 'I haven't mentioned this to you before, Bryce, but the day I arrived here, I very nearly got myself scalded to death in the shower. Who was responsible for that? Miss Erikson?'

Bryce turned an astonished look toward me, and before he could say a word Mrs. Ellett said, 'I don't think anybody was responsible. I think it was just the poor water pressure in the house. Someone, somewhere in the house, must have turned on the cold water for a minute and that's all it took.'

'One of the many things I intend to have repaired around here,' Bryce stated. 'There's no reason why Rosalie and I can't make this our home after we're married.'

I blushed at his words, but this time I didn't care. I didn't even mind that he hadn't asked me. I didn't mind at all!

CHAPTER FOURTEEN

Cora asked us if we'd like to go in for lunch, and as we sat down at the beautifully appointed table, I remembered something else that had been troubling me all along.

'Mrs. Ellett,' I said, 'early this morning when I got up and went down the basement stairs, I stopped at your door and listened and could hear you in there snoring and talking in your sleep. But you weren't there, you said. You, too, had heard something suspicious and had slipped down the front staircase and around in the back to investigate. How could—'

I stopped, noting a sly grin stealing over her weathered face.

'That-there was a tape recording, child. People have accused me of snorin' and talkin' to myself for a long time, so one night I just decided to buy myself a machine and let it play to see if I actually did. Well, I found out, all right. I do snore and mutter, sure enough. So I just kept that tape and thought it might come in handy some time. Then before I slipped on my coat and went out, I set the machine to play back the snores, so I could be gone for a while and nobody would know it.'

'Pretty clever,' Bryce said, and Mrs. Ellett smirked in self-satisfaction at his compliment.

No one had much of an appetite. All of us seemed to be touched by the presence of death in the house, and I was not surprised when Cora asked if it would be all right for her to leave as soon as she had tidied up the kitchen. Bryce told her to go ahead, and suggested that Mrs. Ellett lie down on the couch in the sun parlor for a while. Sam Kuykendall said he would go on back to his trailer, then sort of awkwardly asked Bryce if it would be all right for him to stay there.

'Of course,' Bryce said. 'My grandmother would want you to stay.'

I was glad he had said it, and was equally glad that everybody was leaving, because I wanted to tell Bryce about the message I had received from the pieces of glass.

It didn't take me long to explain about the goblet, the compote, the spoonholder and my hastily jotted notes, although I left out any reference to the question I had about Bryce's trustworthiness. He looked at me with a patronizing expression that showed concern but betrayed his disbelief. 'Oh, come on, now, Rosalie! Surely you can't believe that! You must have accidentally moved the glasses yourself. You know inanimate objects don't move around of their own accord. And it had to be pure coincidence that you happened to notice those particular pieces.'

'I don't care, Bryce,' I said defensively. 'It's true. And it's not that I'm just overwrought, either, although I'll admit that I have been. What about your lavender scented cigarette? Was that just imagination?'

'Uh ... I don't know ... I think I'll quit smoking altogether.' He held out his arms and drew me close. 'Come here, darling. This is where you belong. I meant what I said in the kitchen, Rosalie. You know I love you, and as soon as we decently can, out of respect to Grandmother, let's get married!'

I wanted to say, 'Yes, yes!' but something held me back.

'You don't believe me,' I said.

'I believe you,' he said, but I knew he was just saying it to please me.

'I'll let you know later,' I told him. 'I can never make up my mind about anything right off the bat.' I replaced the Carol goblet, the Viking compote and the Divided Heart spoonholder, straightened all the pieces and locked the doors.

'Everything shipshape?' Bryce asked.

'Yes. That's the way Aunt Francie always wanted it.'

The doorbell was ringing, and as Bryce went to answer it, the telephone rang and I walked into the hall to pick it up. I heard Bryce say, 'Come in, Vernie,' and realized that the man from the mortuary was there, and answered the phone.

'I have a message for Miss Rosalie Bennett,' the voice on the other end said.

'This is she.'

'The U.S. Consulate in Caracas, Venezuela has asked me to inform you that their records indicate Mr. Hobart Willard passed away on September tenth of last year. Are you a relative? The Consulate had no information regarding anyone to contact about Mr. Willard's death until they received your wire.'

'No,' I replied, 'but I will get the information to his son. Thank you for calling.'

Well, I thought, that about winds everything up. Everything except the love I felt for Bryce, and in my heart I was sure that he loved me too, in spite of not believing what I had told him. I told myself not to be ridiculous. To accept his love and his offer of marriage. After all, I had to admit, no one should expect total perfection!

Resolutely I turned and walked back into the dining room and found Bryce standing in front of the Pattern Glass cabinet, staring intently at the contents.

'Bryce,' I began, intending to tell him about the telephone call I had received, 'it isn't easy to tell you this—'

But he held out his arms and I ran to him, my eyes brimming with sudden tears. He held me tightly and then tipped my face up to his and looked into my eyes. 'Can you forgive me?' he said.

'For what?'

'Well, you know. When you told me about the mysterious message that revealed Charlie and Leslie Erikson as being mixed up in some kind of thing, I didn't really believe it.'

'I know.'

'But darling, I do now.'

It was my turn to look at him in disbelief. 'What made you change your mind?'

'Look,' he said, and pointed to the cabinet. On the shelf at eye level were the goblets of the Bryce pattern and the Rose-in-Snow pattern, standing close together. Directly above them, just at the front edge of the shelf, was a spoon holder in the pattern that even Bryce knew was the Wedding Ring. No other pattern carries those distinctive interlocking circles.

'Well?' I gave him an arch look and said, 'Haven't you figured it out that somehow I managed to open the door and rearrange those pieces while I was on the phone in the hall?'

'Please, darling! I deserve that, I know. But you and I were both out of the room, and nobody else has been in there! I was with Vernie Apperson while you were on the phone, and when he left I walked back in here and I know nobody opened that cabinet!'

'Then you believe what I told you.'

'Yes, my dearest love. I do. I believe it. And I love you with all my heart and want you to be my wife.'

'I will, Bryce. And Aunt Francie approves of it, you can see that.' My thoughts flashed back to my item (4)—*Is Bryce to be trusted?* and I realized that this question had been answered, too.

Bryce looked very thoughtful for a second and then said, 'You know, it wouldn't surprise me in the least if Grandmother Quentin hadn't engineered it so as to bring us together in the first place.'

I agreed. And then with a shaky voice I said, 'Look at the top shelf, Bryce. The cream pitcher up there. Do you know what that pattern is? I have an idea it's Aunt Francie's final message to us.'

'I'm not positive,' he said huskily, 'but isn't it named for the little flowers in the design?'

'Yes. It's called Forget Me Not.'

And Bryce and I never will—I'm sure of that.

Photoset, printed and bound in Great Britain by REDWOOD PRESS LIMITED, Melksham, Wiltshire